As If You *Never* Left Me

Katriena Knights

CRIMSON
ROMANCE

F+W Media, Inc.

This edition published by
Crimson Romance
an imprint of F+W Media, Inc.
10151 Carver Road, Suite 200
Blue Ash, Ohio 45242
www.crimsonromance.com

Copyright © 2013 by Katriena Knights

ISBN 10: 1-4405-6783-2
ISBN 13: 978-1-4405-6783-4
eISBN 10: 1-4405-6784-0
eISBN 13: 978-1-4405-6784-1

Chapter One

It had been a good day, and Joely Birch felt about as high as the clouds she could see out her office window. Laughing to herself, she pressed her nose against the glass. The pine-filled valley swooped away, deep down below. She imagined herself suspended above the trees in a hang glider, or perhaps powered by her own wings. She laughed, dizzy with the height and her own happiness, then leaned back and rubbed at the mark her nose had made on the glass.

Joely turned to the computer again, where the graph for her quarterly profit estimate sheet was still displayed. Black numbers all over the place. Compared to last October, business was booming, and last October hadn't been that bad. With the holidays approaching, things could only get better.

She folded her hands under her chin and gazed contentedly at the graph. When she'd left the sprawl of New York City fourteen months ago and settled here, in the sprawling mountains of Colorado, she'd told herself she was doing the right thing. Up until now, she wasn't sure she'd believed it.

From the little gallery's front room, Joely heard whistling. Perry hadn't heard the good news yet, but Joely was sure her one-and-only employee's mood would just get better when she did. The bell on the front door tinkled, indicating a customer had come in, and Perry's whistling stopped. The cheerful sound of her voice rose in its place.

Joely looked back out the window. A lone aspen stood gold against the dark green of the pines. Most of the aspens had dropped their leaves by now and stood reaching empty silver branches to the blue sky. Joely had never seen skies as blue as these, here above the smog, sometimes above the clouds. Today, there were only a few puffy white ones, floating high. It was truly a gorgeous day. Maybe she'd go for a walk later—

"Joely?"

Joely jumped, only then realizing how far she'd let herself drift. Sheepish, she looked up to see Perry grinning at her around the half-open office door.

"Boy, you're in la-la land." She stepped into the room. "I haven't seen you that lost in space since the early, 'Are we ever going to sell anything' days."

Joely laughed. "I have a right to be. Look at this." She moved a little aside as Perry came over to peer at the computer.

"Hot damn!" said Perry as the significance of the graph soaked in.

"That's right. Maybe there'll be a Christmas bonus this year." Joely had no qualms about letting Perry see the spreadsheets—the two of them had spent too many hours alone in this place to have any secrets from each other.

"That wouldn't suck." Perry grinned, then she, too, jerked herself back to the present. "Oh, there's a guy out front who wants to ask you about one of the new pieces."

"Which pieces?"

"Your pieces. The wolf ones you brought in this morning. You didn't give me the rundown."

"Oh, right." Joely had just finished the wolf-themed pots last night, and hadn't had time to make up display cards. "I'll take care of it." She stood, straightening her sweater. "Does he sound interested?"

"Maybe. I told him your more complicated pieces run around two hundred, and he didn't blink. And he's wearing a really nice suit."

Joely paused at the door. "A suit? Nobody up here wears a suit."

"Well, if I had to guess, I'd say he's from out of town. Fine Flatlander Man, we'll call him."

"Fine, huh?" Joely grinned. "Then I guess I'd better hurry."

She stepped out of the office into the space behind the gallery's main display case. The case was full of jewelry, consignment work from local artisans. She sold other items on consignment as well—paintings and sculptures and an exquisite selection of handmade dream catchers. But the centerpiece of her business was the pottery filling the shelves across the room. All that was her own work.

The man perusing her new wolf-themed pieces, his back toward her, was indeed wearing a nice suit. Armani, she decided, at the same time realizing she hadn't had the occasion to identify a suit since she'd left New York. In this area, even the well-heeled tended toward jeans.

In any case, the suit hung nicely across his shoulders. Wide shoulders set atop a tall, lean body. He had brown hair, cut neatly. From the back he looked like—Joely gave a reflexive shudder.

"Good morning," she said brightly. "Perry says you're interested in the new pieces?"

He turned around. For a moment, Joely just stared at him, unable to believe what she was seeing. Her heart took a giant leap in her chest and her adrenaline soared, not sure whether her system should fight or flee or do something else entirely.

His gray-blue eyes regarded her placidly, a smile tugging the corners of his full and inarguably lovely mouth. "Hello, Joely."

Too aware of Perry's lingering presence behind the counter, Joely cleared her throat.

"What are you doing here?"

"Looking at your pottery, apparently."

The familiar voice sent tingles up and down her spine, thoroughly against her will. She hadn't heard it in a very long time, not even over a phone line. Those primal reactions should have died out a long time ago, but apparently they hadn't. Fighting an urge to walk toward him, maybe to touch him—hell, to step right up to him and rip his shirt off, have her way with him right in the middle of the sedate little boutique—she set her mouth in a cold line.

"Are you going to buy it?"

He turned his attention to the sleek, graceful urn, eyeing the howling timber wolf etched on its long curves.

"It's beautiful."

Joely watched his long, clever fingers as they turned the pottery in his hands. She remembered the magic those hands could perform—when he'd bothered to use them.

"Put it down. You're going to break it."

He set it gently on the shelf, the vague smile becoming wider, and soft. "You've really developed your technique. I remember when you still had trouble keeping the clay on the wheel."

"Do you want something, Rey?"

He hesitated, then slowly drew folded papers from inside his jacket. "I want to give you these."

Joely's heart skipped, her mouth going dry. The divorce papers. She'd drawn them up herself fourteen months ago, using software she'd gotten off the Internet, and she'd given them to Rey right before she'd left him. That was the last she'd heard of them.

He held them out to her and she stared at them, afraid to touch them. Even more afraid to touch him, for fear even the accidental brush of his fingers against hers would set off a chain reaction she wouldn't be able to control.

"I finally realized you never filed these, or, as far as I could tell, ever even ran them by a lawyer. Given the circumstances, I thought I should deliver them in person."

She forced herself to reach out, forced her hands not to shake. Careful not to touch him, she took the papers, opened them. Her heart started beating again. She breathed.

"You haven't signed them."

"No. I didn't file them, either, or take them to my lawyer."

"Why not?"

"I guess the same reason you didn't. I didn't want to."

Suddenly exasperated again instead of relieved, she shoved the papers back at him. He wouldn't take them. "It's been over a year, Rey. You called me what, twice? What the hell do you want?"

"I want you to have dinner with me."

Joely spared a glance over her shoulder where Perry still lingered behind the counter. Perry cocked an eyebrow, then slid past the door, back into the office. Joely recognized that expression—she was going to have to bring Perry up to speed, Rey-wise, or suffer the consequences of a bruised friendship.

"Just like that?"

He smiled, bemused. "It's just dinner."

"You came two thousand miles just for dinner?"

"Well, not really."

"Then what do you want really?"

He took a long breath, his attention moving to the papers, still in Joely's hand. "I want to talk. About those, about some other things." His gaze strayed to the office door behind her, as if afraid Perry might come back into the room at any moment.

Joely was having a hard time looking him in the eye, her body betraying her with alarming intensity. She wanted him. Preferably naked, his hands all over her. Wanted him inside her. Hoping for some sort of control, she took a long, slow, careful breath.

"I don't think this is the time or the place," he said.

She swallowed, her heart fluttering again. "No, it isn't. I have work to do."

"Then will you see me tonight?"

The bell on the door tinkled and a woman entered, pausing to look at the jewelry.

"All right. Fine."

"Good." He plucked the papers from her hand and laid them on the counter behind her. "Meet me tonight at that little restaurant next door. Six o'clock. Bring these with you if you want and I'll sign them, then I'll take them back to New York and get them filed. Otherwise—well, I have some things to say."

He turned toward the door, looked back over his shoulder once with a look half smolder and half regret, then he was gone.

It was all Joely could do to keep from running after him. Not fair. So not fair that he could just walk in out of nowhere and light her hormones up like a torch. She was having trouble catching her breath.

Behind her, the office door creaked open and Perry came out, a concerned expression on her face. "I'll take care of the customers," she offered.

"Thanks."

Joely retreated into the office. The computer was still on, a screensaver winding brightly colored patterns across the screen. She pressed a button. The profit graph returned.

She mustered a strained smile. She was doing well on her own. Nothing and no one could take that away, and her heart still warmed at the thought. But everything had changed, because after fourteen months of building life as a single woman, suddenly she was married again.

In the showroom, the bell on the front door tinkled again, signaling the departure of their customer, and Perry came back into the office.

"What's the story?" Perry demanded.

"There's no story." No way was Perry going to let her get away with that, and Joely knew it. She wasn't even sure why she'd tried.

Predictably, Perry cocked her head to one side and regarded her friend dubiously. "You tell me you're divorced, then this long tall drink of water shows up on your doorstep with invalid divorce papers and there's no story?"

Joely put her head in her hands. "Okay, so I fudged things a little. We're not legally divorced."

"So I gathered. And you committed this little oversight because…?"

Joely gave a defeated shrug. "I don't know. I was doing well here, and I didn't feel like dragging up the past."

"You'd think that would be worth your attention, if you really wanted to get rid of the guy."

"I know. I just—I don't know."

Perry leaned against the edge of the desk, crossing her arms over her chest. "That was coherent."

"Yeah. Rey has that effect on me." And other effects, as well, dredging up questions and emotions she'd hoped she wouldn't have to deal with. Ever. She should have known better.

"Rey? That's his name?"

"Reynard. Reynard Birch. Fine Mr. Lawyer Man, we'll call him." Her voice shook a little; she hoped Perry wouldn't notice.

Perry made a face. "He's a lawyer? Defense or prosecuting?"

"Corporate."

"Is that worse or better?"

"It was enough to break up our marriage." She turned her chair, looking out the window. A few puffy clouds had drifted into the sapphire sky scape. Rey didn't belong here. He was part of New York and always would be. She didn't think she could go back to that life.

"You said it's been over a year?" Perry's voice intruded gently on her thoughts.

"Just about."

"He never called or wrote?"

"He called a few times. He wrote some letters. I never read them."

"Why did you leave him?" Her voice had softened a little, and Joely could tell by her expression that she understood how difficult the conversation had become. "Was he abusive?"

"No, it wasn't like that. He just—he had an affair, I guess. With his job."

"So he never beat you, never cheated on you, and never signed the divorce papers."

"That's about it."

"He sounds like quite the ogre." She paused, waiting for a laugh. Joely didn't oblige. "Do you still love him?"

"I don't know." Seeing him had brought back so many memories, for some reason only the good ones. His warm smile. His long, clever fingers. The way his eyes darkened when he came…

Rey still made something inside her sing. Too loudly, even. So loudly it was hard to hear any sort of logic over it. Whether that was love or not, she didn't know. She looked imploringly at Perry. "I don't know what to do, Perry. What should I do?"

Perry shook her head in what appeared to be exasperated sympathy. "Hon, I think you need to go have dinner tonight with your husband."

•••

Joely closed up shop early that evening. It had been another good day, but customers had trickled to nothing by four-thirty, so Joely turned the "Closed" sign around and headed home to face the decision she'd made that afternoon.

She almost wished she'd made him sign the divorce papers right there, just to get it over with. But if he wanted to talk, she supposed she should give him that chance. Could anything he might say make a difference? He'd hurt her so deeply, so irrevocably, that she doubted he could woo her back with words of any kind.

She turned her Jeep onto the dirt road that led to her house, then up the long, winding driveway. Some days, it was too long and winding—days when it snowed, or when a heavy rain washed it into ruts even the Jeep could barely handle. But the payoff was worth it. She pulled into the small garage and headed inside.

The house sat perched on the side of the mountain, looking out over the same sweep of valley she could see out the office window at the gallery. The view was spectacular, but right now, with the sun nearly down, it was hard to see much of anything. She paused by the wide living room windows, trying to pick something out of the shadows. Finally, she sighed and turned on the living room light.

The house itself was small and twenty-five years old, but those facts had brought it within her purchase range. It was little more than a cabin size-wise, but it had electric heat—supplemented by a wood-burning stove to keep the costs lower—water and a septic tank. It also had a satellite dish now, and a hot tub. A cabin supreme. And it was made of logs. Coming as she had straight from New York, that feature had entranced her.

Joely laid her keys on the kitchen table and picked up a silver teapot from the stove. She filled it with water from the sink and turned on the electric stove, setting the water to heat. The microwave would have been faster—water took forever to boil on the electric stove. But today she particularly needed the every-evening ritual. On difficult days, the tea calmed her; on better days it gave her a chance to reflect on everything that had gone right. Today, she would use the time to think about Rey.

In the bedroom, she kicked off her shoes and sorted through the closet. She had no idea what she'd wear tonight, but she certainly wasn't going to face Rey in work garb. Ratty jeans and a T-shirt wouldn't do, either. She wanted to feel sexy but not flaunt it at him. Not too much, anyway. He needed to see what he'd abandoned. Maybe even have his nose rubbed in it a little. After some consideration, she pulled out a bright pink cashmere sweater and crisp, new blue jeans. The sweater clung sweetly to her breasts, and she knew for a fact she looked damned good in a pair of jeans. If that didn't make Rey sweat, nothing would.

Wearing the more casual clothes, she went into the bathroom and straightened her pale, short-cropped hair. Then she wondered why she was making such a fuss. It was Rey, after all, who'd seen her at her best and worst for five years before he'd decided his career was more important than their marriage.

Sudden thickness rose in her throat. She blinked hard as the old emotions rose. The erosion of her marriage had been the most painful thing she'd ever experienced, and the thought of facing that again held her paralyzed for a moment. Could she walk into that restaurant tonight, knowing it could be the first step down a road that led to bereavement?

In the kitchen, the teakettle began to whistle. Joely jerked back to the present, untangling her thoughts from memories of Rey. There was a great deal of good mixed in with the bad. Memories she still treasured, of secrets shared, love whispered, heated bodies tangling in the darkness, or the muted light of late morning. She looked at the mirror, at her own clear blue eyes and the determined set of her jaw.

She had to find out what he had to say.

Chapter Two

With her heart in her mouth, Joely stepped through the front door of the Elk Valley Diner. She paused, taking a deep breath. She'd spent many a lunch break here—the nachos were excellent. It was familiar territory, at least, making her feel less nervous about the impending confrontation with Rey. What could he say to her after all this time? Why had he even come?

Of course, she wouldn't get the answers to these questions until she actually spoke to him. Fighting the urge to turn around and run, she continued into the restaurant.

Rey sat at the bar, sipping a beer. In a chambray shirt and jeans, he looked more like he belonged in Colorado, rather than in a posh New York City boutique. A shock of brown hair fell down over his forehead as he made notations on his phone. Joely found her attention captured by the movement of his fingers. Those fingers could work magic when he put his mind to it, and she could remember the exact sensations, how they felt sliding over her skin, cupping a breast, sliding inside her.

Her attention drifted down lanky, jeans-clad legs to the comfortable-looking hiking boots on his big feet. The jeans were snug but not too tight, displaying each line of his muscled legs and buttocks to perfection. And the feet—although the feet inside the boots were typical knobby man-feet, she had reason to know he lived up to the old wives' tale about the size of a man's feet.

A long, tall drink of water, indeed. She'd forgotten how damn pretty he was. She'd forgotten how much she always wanted him when she saw him. The way he made her breath go shallow and her heart speed up. The way her body opened, ready to take him in.

Gathering herself yet again, she perched on the stool next to him and he looked up, giving her that smile. The one that rendered useless all efforts to calm herself. "Hi." He paused. "So what's the verdict?"

"I don't have the papers."

His face softened with relief, and only then did she realize it had carried the tension of uncertainty. She laid her hand on his, let herself feel the warmth of his skin.

"Why am I here? What do you want to talk to me about?"

"I want a second chance."

She could only stare at him. "I gave you a second chance. And a third chance. A fourth, even. You refused to change anything."

"I know."

His soft admission surprised her. She leaned against the bar. The support helped a little. She felt like her whole world had turned sideways, and if she didn't hold on tight to something, she might fall off.

"I screwed up, Joely. I know that now and I knew it then. I was stubborn and stupid, and I threw away the best thing that ever happened to me." His eyes on hers were soft and sincere. "I want a second chance."

She shook her head, fighting the thickening that had begun in her throat. "I can't go through that again, Rey."

He looked down into the amber of his beer. "I know. I know I have no right to ask. But I'm asking anyway."

Behind them, a waiter called Rey's name, announcing the availability of a table for two. He picked up his beer and slid off the barstool.

"I'd rather discuss this at the table, anyway," he said. "It'll be more private."

"Yes, I suppose it will."

She followed him, using the opportunity to compose her thoughts. The tears hadn't quite gotten underway, but she blinked a few times to be sure they wouldn't plague her. The last thing she needed right now was to break down.

Exactly what kind of second chance was he after? That was the big question. If he thought she was going to pack up and head back to New York with him, he was sadly mistaken.

The waiter settled them in a cozy corner booth that afforded more privacy than she'd expected. That was good. Whatever Rey had to say, they could hash it out here. She didn't want the awkwardness of having him in her house, where it would be too intimate. The booth was discreet but kept him at arm's length. If he managed to get any closer than that, she wasn't sure what she would do. Just seeing him had put him too close to her heart. If he touched her in anything other than a casual manner, all the turbulent, painful emotion inside was likely to explode out of her. So far, she had remained calm. She needed to hold on to that with both hands.

"So," she said after they'd placed their order. "Exactly what are you proposing?"

He leaned over the table, eyes dark with sincerity. Deep, storm-dark. The kind of dark that could drag her in, immobilize her. She swallowed.

"I want a month. A month to be your husband again."

The statement startled her, but she maintained composure. Calmly, she said, "A month is a long time."

"It's barely any time at all. We could have forever together, like we planned in the beginning. A month is nothing."

The tears were lurking again. She fought them and won. "You want me to come back to New York?"

"No. I'll stay here."

"You want to move in with me?" That sounded dangerous. The two of them in her tiny cabin, a chilly Colorado night…If he came to her, she wouldn't be able to tell him no. Part of her heart lurched in anticipation, the other part shrank back in fear.

"Yes," he said simply.

"Where are you going to sleep?"

"I want to be your husband again, Joely."

It took her a moment to form words. This was too much for him to ask—far too much. "That's a bit abrupt after all this time, don't you think?"

He trailed a finger across the back of her hand, over exactly the right spot. Her skin shivered under his touch. She drew a quick breath. The touch shot straight through her, firing every erogenous nerve in her body. No wonder it had been so hard to leave him. "Maybe," he said.

She stared at his hand, at the long, graceful fingers as they traced over her skin, and suddenly she remembered everything. The smell in the hollow where his shoulder met his neck. The tickle of his chest hair against her nose in the morning when she buried her head in his chest. The weight of his arms around her, the weight of his body on her. The firm, slim length of him sliding into her, deep, solid, so far inside her she felt like they had become one person.

She jerked her hand away and tried to rub off the remaining sensation of his touch. She didn't want this, didn't want all this back. "This is a lot to spring on me all at once. I'll have to think about it."

A look of sheepish disappointment rose on his face.

"What?" she asked.

"I don't really have a place to stay tonight."

She shook her head, amazed. "You just thought you were going to ride into town and get me to agree to this scheme right away, didn't you? You thought I'd invite you back into my life—into my bed—with open arms?"

"Well—"

"God, you're arrogant." Fury surged, burning past the arousal he'd lit in her body. Thank God. The arousal had been leading her down a far too dangerous path.

"Or just hopeful."

"No, arrogant." She pressed her lips together, hanging on to her anger like a lifeline. "I know the lady who runs the lodge up the road. I'm sure she can get you a room."

"If that's what you want."

She bristled at his conciliatory tone. "Look, I have a teeny-tiny house. There's no guest room, and the couch isn't exactly huge."

"I don't mind."

"You don't mind now, but you'd mind in the morning when I had to pry you out of it with a crowbar."

He smiled. She was beginning to hate that smile. It made her warm and mushy and hot and needy all at the same time, and that was something she couldn't afford to be.

"You don't want me to stay at the lodge, not if you're thinking about prying me out of your couch."

She drew herself tautly upright in her chair. "It's a very nice lodge. They give you free breakfast with the room."

"I'm sure it's a wonderful lodge."

"Then go there."

"If that's what you want me to do." The smile hadn't faded, and he looked almost smug. She wanted to slap him.

Instead, she eyed him primly. "I think that would be best under the circumstances."

"But you'll think about what I said?"

"Yes, I'll think about it."

He nodded, the smugness fading into something that looked disturbingly like relief. "That's all I ask."

• • •

Back at home, Joely threw her purse on the couch and sat down next to it, staring at the blank screen of her television.

The couch was definitely short. Rey was six feet tall, the couch five-and-a-half. Still, she could picture him curled up asleep on it, his big feet wedged up against one of the arms. Maybe for a few nights, just to see if they could get reacquainted, if they were still the same people they'd been seven years ago when they'd promised to love, honor and cherish.

Snorting at her own naïveté, she picked up the remote and turned on the TV. Of course they weren't the same people. Rey had changed enough during their marriage to rip their relationship apart. And she'd changed, definitely. During their marriage and after it.

But they might still be people who could get along. Maybe even people who could love each other. Certainly the sexual attraction was still there, in a big way. It had been all she could do to keep from playing footsie with him under the table, or taking off her panties and passing them to him, as she'd done a couple of times in college.

She shook her head, disgusted at herself. Sexual attraction wasn't enough—not even close. And it was so intense, so volatile, so consuming, that it was hard to consider anything else over the tumult it produced.

The early news predicted snow for tomorrow. An inch in Denver, which meant the mountains would probably get more. Unless it stalled elsewhere, blew over faster, or moved in an entirely different direction. Typical Colorado weather—tumultuous and unpredictable.

Apparently, that was also typical of her life.

She flipped channels absently for a few minutes, then went into the bedroom to change into her pajamas. The phone on the bedside table seemed to beckon her. She looked at it, took a step toward it, then defiantly stuck her tongue out at it.

The kitchen phone, however, wouldn't be subdued so easily. Against her will, Joely found herself cradling the receiver against her shoulder while the other end of the line rang at the Sky Mountain Lodge.

The lodge's proprietor answered the phone. "Hi, Virginia," Joely said. "This is Joely. I sent someone your way about a half hour ago and I wanted to be sure he made it."

"Oh, yes, the nice young man with the brown hair. Mr. Birch. Is he your brother?"

Joely smiled. "He's my ex-husband. Well, not really ex. Never mind. It's a long story."

Virginia laughed. "It must be, if you sent him here instead of keeping him to yourself. He's a fine one."

"People keep telling me that."

"Well, you let me know when you want him sent back your way. The sign on the wall says I can refuse him service at any time."

"I'll do that." Joely paused, closed her eyes. Maybe the words she felt coming would stop if she concentrated hard enough. "Could you transfer me to his room?" Or maybe not.

"Sure. Just a second."

She could always hang up now, before the call rang in Rey's room. But the phone remained defiantly perched against her shoulder as it rang once, then twice, then half a third time. Rey's voice broke through.

"Hello?"

She closed her eyes against the soft assault on her senses. God, that voice…"Hey, Rey. It's me."

A pause. "Hey, Joely." His voice changed, softened. It sounded furry when he lowered it like that. She hadn't forgotten that, either. The sound set her on fire, heat pouring down her abdomen, spreading over her inner thighs, melting between her legs. At least she was predictable.

"I just wanted to be sure you got settled okay."

"I'm fine. It's a nice lodge."

"I know." She hesitated, questioned her own sanity a couple of times, then said, "Let's get together tomorrow. Lunch?"

"How about breakfast? I know how much you like to eat breakfast out."

"Okay, but it'll have to be early. I open the shop at nine and I like to be there by eight-thirty."

"I'll see you at seven. Do they serve breakfast at that diner?"

"Yes. Good breakfast. I'll see you there."

As she hung up the phone, she wondered where all her common sense had gone. Straight out the window, apparently. But the thought of seeing Rey tomorrow morning over a plate of pancakes made her strangely, warmly happy. It was more than just the arousal, the raw, animal response to him. There was something about him that felt like home, and that was infinitely more dangerous. This was home. She had herself, her business, her log cabin. He was just a distraction, sexy and arousing, and carrying all the baggage of her past.

Crawling into bed, she wondered if she'd responded to him the way she had because she was lonely. She should have gotten herself a dog a long time ago. Then maybe she wouldn't be so vulnerable.

She lay awake for a long time, staring into the empty darkness. Tears pricked her eyelids and she blinked them back.

They had been so good together, when they'd worked at it. She couldn't help remembering. Couldn't push the images back, of their years together, of how perfect it had seemed, before it had all fallen apart.

The first time they had made love, it had seemed like they'd known each other for years. He had touched her as if he knew everything about her. His hands had coaxed things out of her she'd never known existed. Small, wanton sounds, sensations that made her weak, made her weep. She hadn't been a virgin, but she remembered that moment almost better than she remembered the actual loss of her virginity. The sweet, deep shock of him entering her, sliding inside her. Gentle and eager at the same time, wanting to soothe her but also to possess her. He had taken her deep, physically so, but also emotionally. Nothing in her life had ever felt the way it had felt to be made love to by Reynard Birch.

She could have that again. Did she want that again? Knowing everything that could come with it?

She mushed her pillow over her face and swore into it. Damn him, anyway. It wasn't going to be an easy choice, and she had no idea how she was going to make it.

• • •

The Sky Mountain Lodge was nicely appointed and comfortable, but it wasn't where Rey wanted to be. He wanted to be with Joely, in her house, even wedged into her too-short couch. Preferably, though, in her bed. Better yet, inside her.

Instead, he was folding back soft sheets in a room with a rack of elk antlers on the wall above the bed. At least, he thought they were elk antlers. His knowledge of Colorado wildlife was sketchy at best.

He stretched out on the bed and closed his eyes, remembering the way Joely had looked when he'd come into her shop. Still the same tall, willowy blonde girl he'd met in college, with her short-cropped, boyish hair and wide blue eyes. Or maybe not the same, because she wasn't a girl anymore.

He'd missed her so much. It seemed stupid now, that he had closed her out of his life over something as inconsequential as a job.

Of course, it hadn't seemed inconsequential then. It was easy, especially in New York, for priorities to get screwed up. He'd let that happen, and he'd paid for it. Dearly.

He'd been stupid, the kind of stupid only pride could drive a man to. He'd focused on all the wrong things. Hopefully he was focused on the right things now. The most important of those being Joely.

They'd always had a special bond. From the day they'd met, sparks had ignited, and even up to the day she'd left him, a single look had been enough to fan the flames. It had been more than just the sex, too. Though the sex had been incredible. Just thinking about it made him hard. Made him want her so much, he could barely think, or see, straight.

He missed the sex, desperately. He missed everything else about her even more.

With a long sigh, he picked up his phone and turned it on, glancing over his "To Do" list. He could mark one item off—he'd gotten a good look at Joely's pottery. He wondered how hard it would be to get some photos. Probably fairly hard, particularly since he didn't want Joely to know he'd done it. He had to, though, to prove the case he was pursuing. He'd get in touch with his boss in the morning and give him a progress report.

He flipped the organizer closed. He was playing a complicated game here, but he didn't see where he had much choice. As long as Joely didn't figure out what he was up to, he'd be fine. And he'd tell her when he was ready. She'd understand. He was, after all, doing it for her. She stood to benefit a great deal from this case. And maybe it would make up in some ways for the case he'd bungled, the one that had torn them apart.

He set the organizer on the bedside table and turned off the light. As sleep claimed him, he thought not of work, but of Joely. Of her hands on his body, the way she had known how to play him like a fine instrument; fingers, teeth, and tongue, her mouth on him…

In spite of his best intentions, he lay awake for a long time. When he finally did fall asleep, he dreamed of Joely.

. . .

Rey woke the next morning with a headache and a weird, weak feeling. Getting up, he shook with chills, and the room spun around him. He swore, staggering to the bathroom. His stomach dipped and rolled.

Flu, he thought. Some lovely virus being circulated through the jet that had dropped him off in Denver. It figured. He carefully drank a glass of water, then splashed some on his face. That helped a little.

At least he didn't look too bad, judging by his reflection in the mirror. No way was he going to back out of breakfast over some stupid microorganism. He sat back down in the bed to boot up his laptop. The letters on the screen blurred as he composed an email for his boss, saying that he had access to Joely's boutique, and could make a more detailed report later in the week. By the time he was done, he was sweating.

Pulling up in front of the diner, he wondered if he'd made the wrong decision. He sat a moment, gathering himself. He hadn't felt this bad in a long time. Then he caught sight of Joely walking into the diner. His stomach lurched again, only this time he was fairly certain it was arousal. It was hard to tell at this point.

"Joely!" he called, opening the car door. "Wait up."

She paused, smiling, but the smile faded into concern as he approached. Apparently, his appearance had degraded since his last look in the mirror.

She peered into his face. "Are you okay, Rey? You don't look so good."

"It's nothing. A bug or something."

She brushed his forehead, his cheek, and he closed his eyes a moment at the touch of her hand. Sparks again, desire attempting to rise, even through his growing misery.

"You don't have a fever."

"I feel like I do."

She took his hand, drawing him through the door. "Let's sit down."

He followed her without question, grateful to get a solid booth under him. She spoke to the waitress in an undertone while he closed his eyes again, wondering how he could be so dizzy and not have a fever. As he sat down, he realized something seemed odd about Joely. Then it registered—she'd just taken charge. She'd never done that before, not to his knowledge.

A moment later, the waitress deposited a glass of water on the table.

"Drink up," said Joely. "And keep drinking."

"Water?" He drank obediently, though. "Water for the flu?"

"The good news is, it's not the flu. It's the altitude."

"Altitude?"

She gave him a tolerant smile that somehow managed to be affectionate at the same time. "You flew straight out from New York—which is roughly at sea level, by the way—hit 5,280 feet at the airport, then drove straight up the mountain, am I right?"

Rey swallowed water. "More or less."

"We're at a good eight thousand feet here, nine some places. You came up too quickly and now you've got altitude sickness. It happens all the time."

He made a skeptical face. "You're making this up, right?"

"Of course not. When you climb Everest, you have to stop for weeks for your body to adjust to the altitude. Here it takes a day or two, sometimes."

"So what do I do?"

"Drink your water. Rest. Chances are you'll be fine tomorrow."

She laid her hand on his and squeezed it gently. He looked into her eyes and wished he felt good enough to kiss her. "Promise?"

"I promise."

"You're sure you're not making this up?"

"Look it up on the Internet if you don't believe me."

He managed a weak smile and drank more water.

By the time she'd finished her pancakes and eggs—over easy, just like he remembered she liked them—and he'd inched his way through two glasses of water and a piece of dry toast, he was feeling a little better. Not better enough to catch the bill, though. Somehow, she'd paid it and signed the credit card slip before he realized it had hit the table.

"Today's Wednesday," she said. "Business is usually slow on Wednesdays. How about if I call Perry and tell her I'm not coming in?"

"There's no need for that."

"I'd feel better if somebody kept an eye on you today. Altitude sickness can be fatal, you know."

"No way." She had to be making this up.

"Usually just for people who decide to ski or hike a fourteener fresh off the plane, but you've been sitting around in an office so long, no telling how out of shape you are these days."

Her eyes twinkled merrily at his expense. He made a face, not quite energetic enough to inform her he still worked out three times a week. Apparently, that didn't matter up here where there was no air.

"Maybe you should nurse me back to health, then." He had to admit the idea held appeal.

"So we'll leave your car here and I'll drive you back to the hotel."

He agreed, wondering why he was so reluctant to let her take charge, to take care of him, now she had the chance. Just because it had never been that way before, he supposed. He'd always been the one doing the rescuing. Not that he'd been any good at it. So far, she was proving far better suited to the task than he'd ever been. The thought brought a pall over the more pleasant aspects of the role reversal.

Back at the lodge, Joely followed him up the stairs to his room. She tossed her purse on the dresser and made herself comfortable.

"You're staying?" He sat down on the bed and pressed a hand against his throbbing forehead.

"I thought I said that already. I'm going to keep an eye on you until I'm sure you're all right."

He started to shake his head in protest, then reconsidered, blinking back another wave of dizziness. "You were serious? I don't think it's necessary."

"I do." She opened her gigantic handbag. Rey was certain he'd never seen a purse that big before. While she sorted through its contents, he sat there, rubbing his head, clueless as to what to do next. Finally, she looked back up at him. "Take a nap. You'll feel better."

"I'm supposed to just sleep while you're sitting there?"

"Don't worry about me. I'll find something to do." She pulled out a big sketchpad and a handful of pencils and began to arrange them on top of the dresser.

"Yeah," he muttered. He wasn't worried about her finding something to do. He was more worried about himself, sleeping while Joely sat there looking at him. The thought made him feel weird. He couldn't even put words to the sensation.

Then it hit him. Vulnerable. He felt vulnerable. That wasn't a good thing.

Or was it? Time to let go, maybe. Show Joely he still trusted her.

He rubbed his head a few more times, then stripped down to his shorts and climbed back under the covers.

"That's it," she said. Her attention had wandered from her sketchpad and now roved over his body. Her eyes would have undressed him if he hadn't been undressed already. Something stirred in his shorts—he was amazed he was still functioning down there, as sick as he felt. "You just sleep."

He wished fervently that he was up to full health. Up to grabbing her and kissing her and pushing her back into the bed, pushing his hands inside her clothes…"Don't take advantage of me while I'm unconscious."

She smiled. "I'll try not to."

He lay back and closed his eyes. To his own surprise, he immediately forgot Joely was watching him and drifted off, thinking about mysterious mountain-induced ailments and wondering what the hell a "fourteener" was.

• • •

This was nice, Joely decided after the first half hour or so of watching Rey sleep. He'd always been the strong one in their relationship, the one with the better job, the one who could bail her out of situations when they arose. Of course, it had been his miserable failure to bail her out of one such situation that had started their marriage down the crumbling slope of doom.

But now it was her turn to take care of him. He was on her turf here, facing things he knew nothing about. A new experience for him, she was sure. It intrigued her that he'd given himself up to her care so willingly. The old Rey would have fought it tooth and nail.

He slept charmingly—except for the vague snoring—his face mushed into the pillow and one hand curled open next to his nose. She studied his profile, memorizing it. She'd never forgotten it, but it seemed different somehow. Her memory had erased the imperfections, made his nose a little shorter and straighter, his chin a little bigger. Her memory had neglected to remind her he drooled in his sleep.

After a moment, she turned a page in the sketchpad, to a blank sheet. Looking at the familiar lines of his sleeping face, she let her pencil drift over the paper, echoing them, bringing them to existence in soft smudges of gray lead against the white paper. She had drawn him before, a long time ago. Once or twice she had drawn him naked. She was tempted to tweak the sheet away from his shoulders, to expose the long, clean lines of his back, but she didn't want to disturb him. So instead, she drew his wide shoulders, the curl of his hair against the back of his neck, his long nose against the dark pillowcase, his slightly open mouth. She decided to leave out the vague drooling. Not at all aesthetically pleasing.

It felt good to draw him, though. Familiar. The movement of the pencil almost as fulfilling as a caress. She sketched his shoulders, the drape of the sheet over his back, the curve of his skull, his mussed hair. The long, straight line of forehead, of nose, the full, soft mouth. It was like touching him. Like making love to him.

Smiling at the thought, she added one last, small tweak to the line of his chin, then laid the sketchpad aside. She looked at the picture for a few moments, then pulled out her cell phone to call Perry.

"How are things?"

"Quiet," Perry said. "How's Fine Flatlander Man?"

"Very Flatlander-ish at the moment. The altitude knocked him for a loop. Thanks for covering for me."

"No problem. If a man that looks like that ever shows up on my doorstep, I'll expect you to return the favor."

"There's more to a man than looks, you know."

"I know, but it's a nice place to start. Is he going to be all right?"

"Yeah, he'll be fine. He'll probably wake up completely adjusted and ready for a hamburger. I'll drop by the shop as soon as I get him squared away."

"You take your time. And when he wakes up, I suggest you do something creative with him."

Joely laughed. "Thanks, Perry. I'll keep that in mind."

• • •

Rey woke shortly before noon, not quite completely adjusted, but definitely on the mend. The chills had receded along with the vertigo, and the headache had faded to a dull throb behind his eyes. He blinked a few times at the sunlight streaming in through the open window, then turned his head, searching for the vague scratching sound that caught his ears.

Joely sat in a chair next to the bed, her sketchpad balanced in her lap. The pencil in her hand moved fluidly across the paper, drawing long, graceful lines. He couldn't see the picture from here, but the set of her body and the way her hand moved was a work of art in itself. He cleared his throat and she looked toward him, smiling.

"Feeling better?" she asked.

"Much. I guess it wasn't a bug after all."

"I told you." She straightened, stretching her back.

"Let me see."

"What?"

He nodded toward the drawing as he sat up in the bed. "The sketches. Let me see."

She hesitated, then turned the pad toward him. Rough-penciled lines described the symmetrical arcs of a vase, a simple pattern of columbines decorating the curves of its belly.

"It's lovely."

She tilted it back toward herself, looking at it with a crinkle at the corners of her eyes. Being critical.

"It needs a little work."

"They were fools to let you go, back in New York. You could have made that company a household name."

Her mouth tightened. "They might not have 'let me go' if I'd had a better lawyer."

He looked away, stung, and she sagged in her chair. "I'm sorry, Rey. That wasn't fair."

"No, it wasn't."

Standing, she tucked the sketchpad into her voluminous handbag. "As long as you're feeling better, I'm going to head back to the shop. Perry might need the help."

He nodded. "Okay. But don't forget, my car's still at the diner."

"Oh, right. I'll take care of it for you."

He smiled. "I think I like being taken care of."

"Yeah, kind of a novelty for you, isn't it?" Grinning, she headed for the door. "I'll see you later."

"Promise?"

"I promise."

She paused, looking at him, then found herself walking back to the bed. She bent over him and caught his mouth with hers.

She thought she'd forgotten. But as her lips touched his, she was flooded with the taste of his mouth, not only in reality but in her memory. Her closed lips remembered the touch of his tongue, remembered surrendering, opening to let his mouth take hers utterly, but in the real moment, the kiss remained carefully chaste.

This was not an easy thing to do.

After what seemed an eternity of hovering on the edge of complete surrender, she drew back. Looking down into his soft smile, her face went hot. With desire or embarrassment, she wasn't sure. At least he didn't look smug.

She straightened, clearing her throat. "I'll see you later."

This time, she forced herself to leave.

Chapter Three

Perry was helping a customer when Joely entered the shop. She looked up with a question on her face and Joely shook her head, going into the office. She knew Perry was concerned, and Joely hated putting her off, but the customers had to come first. So Joely would have a few minutes to gather her scattered, confused, and admittedly rather aroused feelings before she tried to talk to Perry.

She couldn't believe she'd kissed Rey. She really couldn't believe it had felt so…good. No, so right. It wasn't supposed to feel right. They were supposed to be on their way to a divorce.

"Don't kid yourself," she muttered. She sat at the desk and put her face in her hands. "You should have divorced him fourteen months ago."

"So why didn't you?"

Joely jerked, looking up. She'd been so lost in her own thoughts, she hadn't even heard Perry open the office door.

"I wish I knew, Perry."

Perry sat down in the chair in front of the desk and smiled. "I just sold a four-hundred-dollar necklace. Not your work, but it's a nice commission."

"Wow. The turquoise piece?"

"That's the one." Perry's smile faded into a put-on frown. "I really liked that one."

"You couldn't have afforded it, even with your employee discount."

"Yeah, but what about that Christmas bonus you promised me?"

Joely laughed. "It isn't going to be that big."

"Damn." Perry scooted closer to the desk. "Okay, now tell me what's up with the ex. Oh, wait, he's not technically the ex, is he?"

Joely groaned. "No, he's not. Don't remind me. This situation is difficult enough without having to deal with that particular wrinkle." She pressed the back of her hand to her mouth a moment, remembering the touch of his lips. The taste, the warmth, the flood of memories that had come back to her. "He wants a second chance, Perry. I don't know what to do."

Her voice broke. Perry's expression shifted to one of concern. Joely never cried. Perry leaned her elbows on the cluttered desk. "Do you have any reason not to?"

"The fact he's been across the country for fourteen months and never bothered to make any contact isn't enough?"

"But you said he called a few times, wrote you letters."

"Which I never read."

"Thinking about digging them up?"

"I kissed him."

Perry's mouth dropped open. "What? When?"

"Fifteen minutes ago. Before I left him at the lodge."

"Was it good?"

She closed her eyes a moment. He had tasted so good. "Oh, God, it was fantastic."

"The spark's still there, eh?"

"In spades." She covered her face with her hands again. "Perry, I don't know what to do. I'm so confused."

Perry leaned back in her chair, studying her friend and employer with a sympathetic eye. "You said he wants a second chance. What exactly did he propose?"

"He wants me to give him a month to be my husband again. Totally my husband again. He wants to move into my house." She wrapped her arms around herself protectively. "I'm not sure I want him that close."

Perry nodded. "It seems like a big step, especially after all this time."

Relieved, Joely let out a breath. "You don't think I'm crazy? I mean, being nervous about the possibility of sleeping with my husband?"

"It does sound crazy when you say it that way, doesn't it?"

Joely made a face, but Perry grinned, softening her remark. "No, I don't think you're crazy. I think you're being sensible. I mean, once you sleep with him, you're making some kind of commitment, aren't you?"

"In this case, yes, I think so."

"I think in any case, with you."

Joely sighed. "You know me too well."

Outside in the showroom, the bell on the door rang, indicating the arrival of another customer.

"Things are hopping today," said Perry. "I'm glad you came back. This is nothing like a Wednesday at all."

"Good." Joely stood, nodding decisively. "Customers are good. They'll take my mind off—" She waved vaguely. "—all that other stuff."

But throughout the busy afternoon, as she helped customers pick out gifts for their spouses, their parents, or even for themselves, the memory of Rey's kiss tantalized the edges of her thoughts. By closing time, she'd made her decision.

• • •

After closing up the shop, Joely drove to the lodge, intending to take Rey to the diner to retrieve his car. But the car was already in the parking lot. Puzzled, she went into the lobby.

"Hi, Joely," said Virginia brightly. "How's business?"

Joely smiled at the older woman's typical—and occasionally annoying—perkiness.

"Great, as a matter of fact," Joely told her. "Have you talked to Rey this afternoon?"

"I drove him over to get his car. He seems to be feeling much better." Her lined features took on a dreamy look. "He's such a nice young man. You really should think about not divorcing him."

Joely shook her head, half bemused and half annoyed. "I suppose he's told you all our business?"

"No, not really. Just a little, here and there."

"Just enough for you to feel comfortable doling out advice?"

"Oh, honey, I'd feel comfortable doling out advice on a lot less information than that." Virginia laughed. "I think you know that, too."

"Yes, as a matter of fact, I do." She shifted her purse strap on her shoulder. "I'd better go. I was going to surprise Rey, take him to dinner."

"Go on up, then. You know the way."

So she did, but as she got closer to Rey's door, her feet seemed to forget. Or maybe they were just forgetting how to move. They certainly did slow down appreciably.

Finally, she stood in front of his door. With an effort, wondering where this small, irrevocable move would take her, she knocked.

Rey opened the door. He smiled brightly at her, looking considerably perkier than he had when she'd left him. Considerably better dressed, too. He wore jeans and a cream-colored Irish knit sweater. No shoes, though. She looked down at his big feet in his socks and thought about his toes. He had an interesting trick he did with his toes.

"Hey, Joely. Come on in."

She did, brushing deliberately against him as she passed. Lightly, but deliberately. "You look like you're feeling better."

"Much." He closed the door behind her. "How was your day?"

"Very good. We're selling useless baubles and knick-knacks hand over fist."

"Great to hear." He paused, studying her face. "You have something important to say?"

She grimaced, exasperated. What right did he have to still be able to read her face so well? "Sort of. I thought you might like to have dinner."

"Yes. I haven't had much but noodles and broth today, and I'm starving."

"Noodles and broth? Virginia's secret recipe, I assume?"

"Yes, and very good. It seemed to kill the bug, too."

"I told you, it wasn't a bug, it was altitude sickness."

"And I still think you made that up."

"I didn't, and I'll prove it to you."

"When?"

"Tonight, maybe. I'm inviting you to dinner. At my house."

The air in the room seemed to still as he looked at her, a smile lurking in his eyes, on his mouth. Joely caught her breath. He was like a force of nature, the eighth natural wonder of the world—

"At your house?" he asked.

She forced her expression to remain neutral. "That's what I said. I'll even cook."

He grinned. "Wow. That's big."

"It's huge, Rey. Now come on, before I change my mind."

• • •

Joely pulled into her garage and shut off the ignition. Glancing in the rear-view mirror, she saw Rey's headlights as his rental car stopped behind hers in the driveway.

Unaccountably nervous, as if Rey's opinion actually mattered to her, she got out of the car. He closed his door behind him and headed into the garage.

"And I thought driving in New York was scary," he said.

She snorted. "That wasn't scary. That was fairly tame."

"I'll bet it's scarier in the daytime, when you can see how far the road drops off on either side."

"Actually, it's scarier in the dark, when you can't." She pointed toward the door that led into the house. "This way."

As she led the way, he scanned her small garage with what Joely interpreted as a critical eye.

"It's small," she said, anticipating criticism. Their life in New York had been so different from what she had made for herself here. Of course he would find it strange. "It's just me—I don't need a mansion."

"It's a log cabin," he said, with some wonder in his voice.

She smiled, pleasantly surprised. So that was what had captured his attention. "Yes, it is."

"That's—so cool."

The odd, almost envious glint in his eyes caught her off guard. Rey was a city boy, born and bred—what was he doing getting excited about a log cabin? For a split second, she wondered if she really knew him as well as she thought she did. It was a disconcerting thought.

"I think it's neat." She opened the door into the house, at the same time pushing a button to close the garage door. "I wish I could show you the view. It's fantastic."

"Yeah, it's a little dark right now." Following her into the house, he laid a hand against the curve of her waist and said softly into her ear, "Maybe I'll see it in the morning."

She twisted away from his touch, fighting an instinct to move into his partial embrace. "You'll be back at the lodge in the morning."

"Are you sure about that?" His voice was velvet. She could almost feel it on her skin, like fingers trailing, leaving arousal in their wake.

She turned and fixed him with the best glare she could summon with her blood heating up inside her. "Don't push it, Rey."

Moving past him, she went to the refrigerator and pulled out makings for salad, tossing the head of lettuce onto the cabinet with more force than strictly necessary. Of all the things she didn't want Rey to be right now, arrogant was at the top of the list.

Giving him a dark look through narrowed eyes, she amended that. Sexy was at the top of the list, followed closely by desirable. Arrogant ranked third.

"I'm sorry," Rey said. "I'm a little nervous."

"Nervous?" Arrogant had just been kicked to fourth place by adorable. "Why would you be nervous?"

"Why wouldn't I be?"

"This was your idea, Rey. If it's not working, maybe you should back out."

The red bell pepper she'd just put on the cutting board rolled off and hit the floor. Rey picked it up and put it back, coming uncomfortably close to her again as he stepped closer to the kitchen counter. "Is there anything I can do to help?"

Exasperated, Joely pulled a knife out of a drawer and set to work on the head of lettuce. "I don't know. See if you can find the chicken in the fridge."

There was silence for a time as Rey pulled out the thawed chicken breasts and a pair of tomatoes. He helped himself to another knife and a cutting board, and within minutes they were following an old rhythm, one worked out over practice in the kitchen of their first apartment where the space had been limited, she cutting veggies for the salad, he assembling chicken cacciatore in a skillet on the stove. He swiped a handful of her chopped bell peppers, a handful of her mushrooms. She passed him a bottle of oregano before he asked for it.

It wasn't until that moment, when his fingers touched hers on the bottle of spice, that she realized what was happening. How automatically it had happened. Old rhythms, picked up as if not a day had passed, much less over a year. She swallowed hard, thinking about the implications. About other rhythms, other rituals. His body and hers, moving together, taking, giving—

She didn't pass him the basil until he asked. Twice.

• • •

"Just like I remembered it." Rey pushed his chair back from the table, leaving a scraped-clean plate behind. He meant everything had been just like he remembered it, not just the chicken cacciatore, which admittedly had more going for it in terms of sentiment than in gourmet quality cooking. But the way they'd cooked it…

Joely swept up his plate as well as her own, carrying them to the sink. "Glad you liked it."

"Remember when we used to both get home from work and make that for dinner?"

She didn't look at him. "Yeah, I remember."

He smiled, taking advantage of the fact she couldn't see him. He got the impression she was remembering a lot of things. That was good. He wanted to remind her of the good times, so she could forget the bad times. And do the same for himself. When he remembered what he had done, how he had, in so many ways, just thrown her away, it hurt. He wanted to stop hurting.

But what should his next move be? He didn't want her to get dinner wound up and decide it was time for him to leave. Desperately scanning the living room, his attention lighted on a CD player on a shelf by the TV. "Music?"

"Sure, why not." She sounded like she hadn't even heard him.

He picked out a CD from the stack next to the player—a female artist whose name he didn't recognize. The music started with a soft arrangement of guitars. That would work. He let it play and sat down on the couch.

"Leave the dishes," he said. "Come sit down."

She turned off the tap. Bubbles had risen in the sink. "You're going to do the dishes later?"

"I just might. It seems fair, doesn't it?"

She almost smiled. He saw it form at the corner of her mouth, then watched regretfully as she caught it and forced it back where it had come from. But she left the dishes, and sat down beside him on the couch. Stiffly, though, and as far away from him as she could manage.

"Thanks for dinner," he said.

"Dinner's not much."

"It was plenty."

She softened a little, her stiff spine relaxing. She seemed closer to him suddenly, though she hadn't changed position on the couch. She started to speak, then looked away. Finally she said, "I missed you."

"I missed you, too." He paused, watching her profile as her mouth, too, released much of its tension. "Once I got my head out of my ass and realized what I'd done."

She laughed lightly, the sound almost hiding the pain he knew lay behind it. "Took you long enough."

He edged toward her, his arm along the back of the couch. "Why didn't you answer any of my letters?"

"Because I never read them."

That stung. "Why not?"

She took a moment to answer. He thought he saw a crystalline glint in her eye, a tear poised on the edge of her lower lashes. "Because I knew how much it would hurt."

He could say nothing to that. He'd caused that hurt, and in that moment, he realized how monumental a thing it was for him to ask her to forgive him. How could he have believed it might be possible? Was he really that arrogant, to think she could let go of all that pain, just to have him back?

But he leaned closer, because he also realized how empty he'd become over the last two years, how much he needed her. In the background, the music had become more strident, the female vocalist singing harsh words against a former lover. Appropriate, he thought, though he'd hoped for something sweeter. Joely seemed not to notice.

His eyes drank in her face, the porcelain skin flushed with emotion, the distant, ice-blue eyes. "I love you," he said. He hadn't meant to.

She turned toward him and the glitter of tears overflowed onto her face. "Oh, Rey, don't hit me with that. It's not—"

He didn't give her a chance to explain what it wasn't, because his body, moving apparently of its own volition, closed the distance between them. His mouth caught hers, molded itself to her familiar shapes. A small sound rose in her throat and he pressed closer. His hands curved against her waist.

She didn't pull back. She didn't know why she didn't pull back— God knew she should have. But the taste and the movement of his mouth against hers were too good, too beautiful. Her mouth opened under his as it had so carefully refused to before, at the lodge. She let him inside.

She moaned as his tongue tangled with hers, soft but insistent, stoking a flame that burned all through her body. It had been a long time since she'd felt that kind of heat. She'd never felt it with anyone but Rey.

Stop. Stop now before it gets any worse.

Or should that be any better…She was utterly confused by now. So confused that she did nothing when Rey's hands slid up along her sides, then forward to cup her breasts. He pressed against her, thumbs finding her nipples. So familiar, the heat and the shape of his hands on her, caressing and arousing her breasts. The smell of his hair as he shifted, burying his face in her neck. His tongue traced her neck from her shoulder up to the curve of bone behind her ear, as desire moved hot and liquid through her body, pooling between her legs in familiar, wet arousal.

A voice intruded. Raspy and feminine, it sang, "You were wrong wrong wrong, then you were gone gone gone," with a background of darkly strumming guitars.

Joely pushed herself back, her heart beating so hard it made her dizzy. "That's enough, Rey." Her words didn't sound as forceful as she'd intended. In fact, they sounded almost plaintive, as if she'd said, "Please don't stop," instead.

But he let go of her and leaned back as she rose from the couch to walk back into the kitchen. "I'll just do the dishes," she said. "You can turn on the TV or something, if you like."

The CD was still playing, though. Rey made no move to turn it off, in spite of the imprecations the singer was hurling at her ex. She dared a glance over her shoulder. He just sat there, staring at her.

"Maybe you should go," she said.

"I can't." He grinned sheepishly. "The lady at the lodge says I'm not welcome back. I'm not sure what I did, but it must have been bad."

Thin-lipped, Joely stared down at the dirty dishes. *You engaged Virginia's imagination.* "I'll call her. I'm sure I can change her mind."

There was a long pause, almost long enough to make Joely look up, but she stared resolutely at the sink. Finally Rey said, "Are you sure that's what you want to do?"

She stirred the soapy water with her hand, watching the detergent bubbles cling to her skin. "No. You can sleep on the couch."

Behind them, the jilted lover sang, "And when you came back, I just kissed you and said hello again."

Chapter Four

Rey offered to help Joely with the dishes, but she told him no. She had no desire to have him that close to her for more than two or three seconds at a time, for fear she might do something she would regret. Like pull off all his clothes and rub herself all over his naked body. So she told him to relax and not worry about the dishes. He stayed on the couch, and when the CD had run its course, he turned on the TV.

Listening to him flip channels, Joely had a thought. "Where's your luggage?"

"In the trunk of my car."

She wiped the last plate dry. "You should probably go get it, then, if you're staying."

He twisted sideways, looking at her over the top of the couch. His gaze scanned her face, searching. She wasn't sure what he wanted to see. Schooling her features—except for an eyebrow that insisted on quirking upward—she met his scrutiny evenly.

"You at least want a toothbrush or something," she said finally.

Whatever he'd been looking for on her face, he must not have found it, because now he looked disappointed. "Yeah. Probably."

He rolled off the couch and walked toward the door. She yanked the plug out of the bottom of the sink and stood for a moment watching the water drain. When it had finally emptied, she dried her hands and went back into the living room.

The couch was still warm where he'd been lying. She laid her hand on the warm space and sat still for a moment. His smell lingered. Reluctantly, she drew her hand away and moved to the other end of the couch. She'd just settled into a spot when he came back in, lugging a large suitcase and a smaller computer bag. He set them down next to the couch.

"So this is my room?" The corner of his mouth twitched.

"Yes."

He sat next to her. She stood up, to get away from his warmth, his smell, all the temptation they sparked in her. "I'm going to bed."

"It's eight o'clock," he said, dubious.

Joely got the feeling Rey knew exactly why she was trying to leave. "I'm tired," she protested weakly.

He pointed at the TV. "I thought you liked this show."

Joely hesitated, surprised he remembered. "Well, I—"

"Just sit down and watch it. I won't bite."

"I'm not worried about getting bitten." Although biting wasn't necessarily a bad thing…

He shrugged, his smile not quite smug. "Okay, I won't touch you, then."

That hit closer to the root of the problem. She waffled again, then gave in and sat at the far end of the couch. Which still didn't leave much room between them. She could still smell him, could feel his warmth if she concentrated a little. She really needed a bigger couch.

He kept his promise, though, and gradually her unease faded. Fifteen minutes later, they were laughing companionably over the antics of the familiar characters. They'd always enjoyed watching TV together, though usually they'd sat much closer together, close enough she could feel his laughter before it started. Even now, with the distance between them, she felt some of the same camaraderie. Especially since they both still laughed at the same jokes. Maybe there was a chance, after all.

She forced her thoughts away from maybes, and made herself concentrate on the television. Finally, about halfway through the late news, she found herself yawning.

"Tired?" Rey asked.

"Yeah. And I have to get up in the morning to go to work." She headed for the hall closet. "Let's get that bed made up."

"Just toss me some blankets. I'll take care of it."

That worked. If he made up the couch himself, she wouldn't have to help him. Wouldn't have to stand shoulder-to-shoulder with him thinking about the two of them together in bed, under sheets, over sheets, tangled in them.

No, much better if he did it himself. So she tossed him sheets, a blanket, a quilt and a pillow from the hallway. He caught them, looking bemused.

"I don't need this many blankets."

"That's what you think, city boy." She tossed him another blanket. "Weren't you watching the weather?"

"Yeah. Do you really think it'll snow tonight? It's only October."

"Snow in October is par for the course in Colorado." She closed the linen closet. "There are more blankets in here if you need them." With that, she turned and left him standing there alone, arms full of blankets.

Alone in her room, she changed into her purple flannel pajamas. Not exactly sexy, but certainly warm.

Now why in the world would you need sexy pajamas? It's not as if he's going to come in here and take them off you. She rolled her eyes at her own wandering thoughts and crawled into bed.

But, in spite of nearly drifting off during the news, now she couldn't sleep at all. She lay awake looking at the ceiling, thinking about Rey in the other room. He'd never slept in more than a pair of boxers; she doubted he had on anything more right now. Maybe he was asleep already, hair tousled, drooling on the pillow.

How had he managed to get past her barriers so quickly? She'd been determined to protect herself, and now here he was in her house, sleeping in his underwear on her couch only a room away.

All this after fourteen months, during which he'd barely tried to contact her…

She sat up suddenly, tossing back the covers. On the shelf in her closet was a white shoebox she could barely reach. Straining upwards on her toes, she caught hold of it and managed to maneuver it down into her hands.

She carried it back to the bed and covered herself back up, tucking the blankets around her lap. She let the house get quite cool at night, to keep her electric bill down and to prevent having to keep more than a small fire burning in the stove. So, before she opened the box, she made sure she was cozy.

Even then, she stared at the box's lid for a time before she finally pushed it open. Inside were twelve letters. Unopened, addressed to her, in Rey's handwriting.

He'd tried. He'd called her several times, as well. He'd even called her mother to track down her phone number, and Joely knew he'd rather have dental work done than talk to his mother-in-law. She'd never opened his letters, and had used Caller ID to avoid his calls.

What had she been afraid of? Had she thought maybe he would say something that would change her mind? Why hadn't she given him a chance, back then?

She picked up the top letter and slid her index finger under the envelope's flap. There was a small tearing sound. She stopped. For a moment, she sat frozen like that, the tip of her finger ready to tear the envelope open. Then she put the letter back, closed the box, and stuffed it under the bed.

Whatever she'd been afraid of then, she was afraid of the same thing now. Afraid of opening herself up again, of getting hurt.

Or maybe she was just afraid it was too late.

She lay there, curled up in the blankets, curled around her heart, remembering what it had been like to have him next to her in bed, just sleeping, his warmth suffusing the blankets. A man in bed could come in handy on those cold mountain nights. The altitude sucked the heat out of the air even in the depths of the summer. And he was just down the tiny hallway, wasting all that glorious male heat on her couch cushions.

Resolutely, she grabbed her spare pillow, wrapped her arm around it and closed her eyes. She'd slept alone in this bed for fourteen months, and she'd stayed plenty warm enough. She would be fine.

• • •

The couch was too short. Way too short. Rey butted his feet up against the armrest, but his head was still squished against the other one. He could put his head on top of the armrest, but it was uncomfortable, digging into his neck and squishing his ear. The pillow helped, but not enough.

He was never going to get to sleep at this rate. Adding to his frustration was the thought that Joely was only a room away in a perfectly comfortable bed that undoubtedly had more room for him in it than this stupid couch did. He'd even promise not to touch her, if he could just get enough room to stretch out flat on his back.

Who was he kidding? He could promise, but he'd touch her anyway. As much as possible. Maybe it would be better for them both if he just stayed here.

Maybe if he had another pillow…

He sat up, peering down the short hallway. A small nightlight burned next to the bathroom door, which was good because otherwise the tiny house was pitch black. He'd never lived anywhere without streetlights, and the immensity of the darkness here had caught him off guard. There must not be any moon to speak of tonight. He'd never thought much about that, either.

Joely's bedroom door was closed. He hadn't heard anything from that part of the house since he'd finished tucking himself in. She'd probably dropped right off to sleep, sprawled all over her comfortable bed. He wondered if there was another pillow stuffed into that miniscule linen closet.

He pushed back the blanket and quilt and tiptoed across the room, feeling gooseflesh crawl down his back. The chill had surprised him, as well. It had been fairly warm today, and he hadn't expected the temperatures to drop off as much as they had. Another one of those weird mountain things, he supposed.

He was shivering by the time he got to the linen closet. Carefully, he turned the knob and opened the door. It squeaked a little and he grimaced, looking toward Joely's door. Surely she hadn't heard that. He poked his head into the closet, squinting in the darkness, and made out the lump of a pillow.

"Aha!" he whispered, and dragged it out. It had a pillowcase on it and everything. What luck.

He saw the shadow move out of the corner of his eye. It was a person, and it wielded something large and probably dangerous. He wheeled automatically, lifting the pillow to protect himself.

"Get out of my house! What the hell do you think you're doing in my house?" The screeching voice was barely recognizable as Joely's. Rey cringed, waiting for her to hit him, but whatever she had, she was only brandishing it.

"Joely! Joely, it's me!" He peeked around the edge of the pillow. She barely had her eyes open.

"Get out get out get out—" Her litany suddenly broke off. She shook her head and lowered her weapon, which proved to be a golf club. She reached toward the wall switch, and a moment later, the hallway was flooded with light. Cautiously, Rey lowered the pillow.

Joely regarded him with bleary eyes, blinking against the sudden light. "Oh," she said. "Sorry."

He looked at the golf club in her hand. One of his old Big Bertha wood drivers, if he wasn't mistaken. "Good God, Joely, you could have killed me with that thing!"

To her credit, Joely looked chagrined. "I said I was sorry. I was having a dream and I heard you in the hallway and I woke up. I'm not used to having somebody else in my house."

"No wonder, if this is the way you treat your houseguests." Suddenly, he realized there was more of interest here than his old golf club—and he'd been wondering for a while where that had gotten off to. Joely had on dark purple flannel pajamas. Sexy ones, with lace trim around the neck and sleeves. The top button had come undone and Rey could see the inside curves of her breasts. She looked tousled from sleep, much as she'd used to look after sex. Except for the red sheet marks on her face, but that didn't detract from the effect enough to stop Rey's cock from springing to abrupt attention.

He was at a great disadvantage, standing there in nothing but a pair of white cotton briefs. Joely, apparently seeing the shift in his gaze, looked right at his crotch.

"Forget it, Rey." She spoke the words directly to his burgeoning erection, which ignored them completely. Then she spun on her heel, dragging Rey's golf club behind her, and went back into her bedroom.

"God, this sucks," said Rey, and headed back toward the couch. He should have known better than to think he could be this close to her without suffering for it. He wanted to be with her, not just near her.

Now he'd never get back to sleep.

• • •

There was no sleeping for Joely, either. She lay awake in bed, tossing and turning, smashing and re-smashing her pillow, muttering to herself and generally becoming thoroughly involved in an intense case of insomnia.

She couldn't get the image out of her head—of Rey in nothing but his underwear, erection straining against the thin cotton. She had been able to see every detail—the curve of it, the demarcation between shaft and head. She hadn't seen him that thoroughly aroused since a few months after their honeymoon. Standing there in the cold hallway, she'd wanted to put her hand right under the straining cotton of his fly and go to town. If she had, she'd probably be sleeping right now, satiated and snoring.

Instead, she was all alone in a big bed, punishing her pillow for her own stubbornness.

A month, he'd said. There was no way she could have him in her house for a month and not drag him, at some point, straight into her bed, get him naked and have her way with him. So she had to decide, and soon, whether to go along with his plan. To let him be her husband again, in thought, word, and deed, or to send him packing back to New York.

She smashed her pillow again and looked at the clock. Four hours from now, she had to get out of bed and go to work. Maybe Perry could tell her what she should do. She had a feeling she knew exactly what Perry would say.

Closing her eyes, she pictured again the clean lines of his bare torso, remembered what his skin felt like under her hands. Remembered what it had been like to make love to him, to let him inside in every possible way. The thought of sending him away brought tears to her eyes. So did the thought of letting him stay.

She looked at the clock. Three A.M. It was going to be a long night.

· · ·

To her own surprise, she did eventually fall asleep, which she discovered when the ringing phone woke her. Barely conscious, she rolled over and picked up the receiver on her bedside table.

"Joely, I know you're not awake," said Perry before Joely could jump-start her voice. "Just look out the window."

Joely rolled half over to peer over the headboard of her bed, tweaking the curtain aside. "Oh, my God." Her tone was more reverent than upset.

"Yep. Don't bother coming in. I'll call Virginia and tell her we won't be there."

"Okay. Thanks, Perry."

She turned the phone off and leaned her chin against the headboard, looking out at nearly eighteen inches of snow. And it was still coming down, so thickly she could barely see the small barn that held her studio, only twenty yards or so from the house.

Smiling, she settled in to watch for a while. She loved to watch the soft drifting of snow from the low, gray clouds, piling silently in her yard, filling the valley with white. It made her want to sing "White Christmas," even though it wasn't even Halloween.

A sudden noise interrupted her reverie. Startled, she started to reach for the golf club, then remembered. Rey. How could she have forgotten? Especially after she'd nearly brained him last night. And standing there looking at him in his skivvies... Sometimes her brain amazed her with its ability to forget things. Self-preservation, she supposed, particularly in this case.

She swung her feet out of bed and stuffed them into her fluffy slippers. The wooden floors would be cold. Grabbing her heavy, terrycloth bathrobe on the way out, she went to check on Rey.

She found him a little sooner than she'd expected. He was in the bathroom, occupied. The door, which had a bad latch and loose hinges, was slowly swinging open.

Joely couldn't resist a look. He was still in nothing but his shorts, shivering visibly. Unfortunately, he had his back turned to her, making it impossible for her to see what he had in his hands. That was too bad.

"Getting a little casual, aren't we?" she said.

"I closed the door," he protested.

"You have to pull it shut pretty hard. The latch doesn't always catch."

"Well, I wouldn't know that, now, would I?"

Joely smiled. Rey seemed almost embarrassed. That would be a new experience for him. "Shall I close it?"

"Yes, please."

Obligingly, though reluctantly, she shoved the door closed, making sure it stayed closed this time.

In the kitchen, she started water for tea, reflecting on how nice it was to have time to linger over it. She stoked the fire in the stove, as well—something else she rarely bothered with in the mornings, because she usually headed straight to work. It felt good, though, to hold her hands in the growing warmth and think about nothing. Nothing to worry about today, no plans to make, nowhere to go. Maybe she could work on some of those sketches she'd started, though it didn't look like she'd be able to get to the workshop—

Then it hit her. She was going to be stuck in this house all day. With Rey.

This was not necessarily a good thing.

The bathroom door squeaked and Rey came back out. There was a strange cant to his gait. It was the contorted, uncomfortable walk of a man too macho to let himself shiver. He made his way into the living room and sat on the couch, kicking open his suitcase.

"At least it's warmer in here," he muttered, then did a double take, squinting at Joely. "You're not dressed. Don't you have to go to work?"

"Look out the window." In the kitchen, the teapot whistled. Joely went to answer its call.

Rey pulled on his jeans, then picked up a sweatshirt and went to the sliding doors leading to the small deck. He opened the blinds and stared.

"When did that happen?"

"Last night. It was in the weather forecast. Would you like some tea?"

Shaking his head, he continued to gape at the backyard, as if the snow might disappear if he looked at it long enough in disbelief. "They said two to three inches. This is closer to two feet."

"Not quite. Do you want tea, Rey?"

Joely left a cup for Rey on the kitchen counter in case he wanted it and walked back into the living room with her own tea. "That was the Denver forecast. We're not in Denver."

He yanked his sweatshirt on, then grabbed a pair of socks from his suitcase. "So you're just going to stay home and lose a day of business? Can you afford that?"

She shrugged, checking the stove. It was heating up nicely. "It's a snow day. Like school. Nobody's going to be out shopping for knick-knacks in this, anyway."

"I guess that's true." He looked at the stove, then held his hands out to it casually, as if he were just experimenting instead of desperately searching for some kind of warmth. Joely hid her smile behind her teacup. "Is there any coffee?" Rey went on. "I could use a cup."

"I made tea," said Joely. "Have you not been listening to me? And there's a cup on the counter."

"Oh. Okay."

He went into the kitchen to retrieve his tea.

• • •

It hadn't quite registered with Rey until this morning how small Joely's house really was. He'd thought maybe there was another bedroom or a study or something lurking around a corner, but there wasn't. Kitchen, living room, bedroom, bathroom, deck, garage. That was it. Oh, and that tiny linen closet.

That was good, though. Because it would be extremely hard for her to get away from him.

Things had already gotten comfortably domestic. He helped himself to cereal out of the cupboard while she drank her tea and ate toast with that all-fruit jelly she'd always liked. She thumbed through a magazine while she ate, not talking to him but not really ignoring him, either.

The whole scenario was far more comfortable than he'd expected.

"So what do you usually do when you're snowed in?" he said suddenly. The silence was comfortable in its way, but it was starting to worry him. He'd never get anywhere with his planned seduction if they just sat around doing their own thing all day.

She looked up from the magazine. "I thought I might work on some sketches. It'll be hard to get to the workshop through the snow. Once it settles down a little, Rob from up the road will come by with his snowplow and clear the road and the driveway."

"Really. Rob, huh?" Was Rob a new wrinkle in the situation?

"Yeah, the whole neighborhood pays him a sort of retainer, salary, whatever, and he clears all our driveways for us, plus the road. The county doesn't maintain this stretch."

"I see." When you lived in the middle of nowhere, he supposed, you had to come up with arrangements like that. Heaven forbid the city or county or whatever would do it for you. He thought about the big snowplows that cleared the streets at home, and about alternate side of the street parking. That kind of thing probably wouldn't work on these narrow, winding roads.

Sipping his own tea, he looked at the black, wood-burning stove and wondered if she'd ever tried to cook anything on it. "It's like a whole different world out here, isn't it?"

She shrugged. "In some ways. But it's really not all that strange." She turned back to her magazine.

Not that strange. She had to burn wood to keep her house warm, and pay somebody to plow the road. Her house was made of logs, and the TV weatherman couldn't predict the weather for her piece of his viewing audience. No, this wasn't strange at all. Hell, it was so much like New York City, who could tell the difference?

Chapter Five

Joely sat at the kitchen table and sketched for a time, trying to pretend Rey wasn't sitting across from her. Not the easiest task.

He'd gotten his computer out and connected to her wireless so he could catch up with the news. Apparently, the idea of trudging down her driveway through eighteen inches of snow to get the paper didn't appeal to him. Of course, that was assuming the paper was even there. Given the conditions, Joely suspected it wasn't.

So, between the scratching of her pencil and the tapping of his keys, they filled the silence companionably.

It didn't seem right, though, to sit and say nothing. There were fourteen months of silence between them already—shouldn't they find some way to address that?

"What are you working on?" Rey said suddenly.

Joely tweaked a line she'd been fussing over before turning the sketchpad to show Rey. He perused the picture. "Nice. This goes with the one you drew at the hotel."

She nodded. Finally happy with the vase she'd sketched, she'd tried variations of the columbine design on a bowl and mugs. "I like to do things in sets. Sometimes somebody even buys them all together."

He nodded thoughtfully. "And yet they work as single pieces as well, so if somebody only buys one, you can still sell the rest."

"That's the plan." She turned the book back around, eyeing the drawing again. "These mugs I'll probably price as a set of four, though."

"You know what you need?"

There was a loaded question. "A million dollars?" *A good lawyer in tight blue jeans?*

He plowed past her joke. "You need somebody to handle the financials so you can concentrate on the creative end of the business."

"If I had a million dollars, I could hire someone."

He opened his mouth, but closed it again, an oddly disappointed look on his face. She had the strangest feeling he'd been about to volunteer for the job. Instead he picked up his laptop and put it back into its case.

She found herself watching him, her eyes fixed on the sure movement of his long fingers. She'd always loved those hands. He pulled the zipper shut and pushed the computer case aside, bumping it up against the end of the couch.

Something in her throat started to burn. She swallowed hard before it could turn into tears. "I shouldn't have said what I did," she said abruptly.

He looked up, puzzled. "When?"

She swallowed. "Last August."

The puzzlement faded from his face and he nodded slowly. "I probably would have come after you sooner if you hadn't."

There was no answer for that. When she spoke again she spoke to his hands, unable to meet his eyes. "I was angry."

"You don't say." His mild tone caught her off-guard. When she looked up, he had a quirky smile on his mouth. "I never would have guessed."

She returned his smile, sadly. "We have a lot of things to talk about."

"Do we?"

"I think so, yes."

"We can't just…forget about it and move forward?"

"I don't think I can, no." No matter how hard it might prove to be, she didn't think she could consider a future with him without working through their past.

His gaze slid sideways, and she could tell he was disappointed by her answer, but he shrugged, resigned. "Okay, then, we might as well dig in." Folding his hands in front of him on the table, he added, "You first."

Her eyes widened. She hadn't expected that. Where in the world was she supposed to start? Of all the wounds they'd inflicted on each other, which should she pick open first? Rallying, she said the first thing that came to mind. "Why did it take you so long to come after me?"

He nodded approvingly. "Okay. A tough question, but fair."

"You're stalling, Rey."

"Yes, I am."

Resting her chin on her fist, she waited while he gathered the pieces of his answer. Would this be the honest Rey, who'd bared his soul to her from time to time? Or Rey the equivocator, whom she'd seen wowing the jury in court? Or attempting to wow the jury. She still couldn't shake the image of the last trial of his she'd witnessed, when all attempts at wowing had failed miserably.

"When you left—" he started, then broke off, shaking his head. "I don't really want to go into this. It can't help. We both know what happened."

Joely blinked back sudden, surprising tears. She remembered it all too well. Inwardly, she cringed to remember the imprecations she'd thrown at him along with the divorce papers. *"Don't bother calling me, Rey. It's too late to fix this. If I never see you again, it'll be too soon."* And that had been the least of it. She hadn't thought about that in a long time. She'd shoved it into the back of her mind so she could pretend it had never happened. A part of her still refused to believe she could have been so awful to him. So hateful. Hurtful.

His gaze caught hers as she regained control of her swimming eyes. His pain was masked there, but she could still see it lurking.

Maybe he was right. It would be like picking at a nearly healed wound to revisit those moments.

"It occurs to me," he said slowly, "that you might have some of the answers you need if you'd taken the time to read my letters."

She swallowed. The letters. She hadn't wanted to read them last night, and she didn't want to read them today. But maybe he was right. Maybe she'd missed what she'd needed to hear, back then, by not looking at them. A wave of nervous tension suddenly passed through her, making her almost nauseated. Better to get it done, if he was going to insist. Like pulling off a Band-Aid. Make it quick.

He wasn't sure why he brought up the letters. He already knew she hadn't read them—she'd told him that in the restaurant. But when she got up and walked into the bedroom, he had a sudden sense that it had, in fact, been the right thing to say.

She came out carrying a shoebox, which she set on the table next to him. Tentatively, she sat back in her chair, crossing her arms tightly over her chest. He waited for her to say something, but she didn't. So he opened the box.

They were all there. All the letters he'd written her after she'd stormed out of their apartment. Running his fingers over the edges of the envelopes, he counted twelve. None had been opened. Was that really all there'd been? He could have sworn he'd written at least a hundred. He looked up at Joely.

"Read them," she said. "Or shall I?"

He cast his mind back and dredged up some of the more colorful contents of the letters. "I'll read select highlights under one condition."

"What's that?"

"I burn them when I'm done."

Her eyebrows shot up into neatly plucked, pale blonde arcs. "That bad?"

"Some of it."

She considered. She looked almost frightened. "All right. It's a deal. Read."

He opened the first envelope, unfolded the letter, and confronted his own, old pain. If he let his guard down even a little, he could feel it burning a straight line down the middle of his chest, as if someone had sunk a knife there. He cleared his throat. "'Dear Joely,' blah blah blah, 'I can't believe you're running to Colorado. Why don't you just go all the way and head for L.A.?'"

"That was cold."

"A little." He went on. "'Are you sure this friend of a friend with the storefront up for sale is legit? You have no idea what you're doing and you could get screwed over big time.' See? I was concerned for your welfare."

"Nice."

"Yes. 'Also, where the hell is Bailey, Colorado, anyhow?'" He paused, skimming a few paragraphs. "'I don't want you to be in Colorado. I want you back here where you belong. And if you think I'm signing those divorce papers, you're fricking nuts.'"

"Does it really say 'fricking'? You're not censoring?"

"Not that part."

"You skipped a lot."

He winced, thinking about some of the harsh words he'd skipped as he'd read. "Just filler." He put the letter back in the envelope and set it out of her reach.

As he opened the second letter, he wondered again why he'd decided to do this. Each letter was like a window into the past, allowing him to relive the brutal, searing emotion he'd poured into each one. It hurt.

So he continued to read aloud, a sentence here, a paragraph there, just until he saw on her face that she understood. That was all he wanted. Just for her to understand why he hadn't pursued her more diligently. Why he was only here now, fourteen months later.

I won't chase you halfway across the country if you don't still love me. There's no point. Give me some sign I should come and I will. Because I still love you. That's not going to change.

Five letters on the pile.

If you meant what you said, I don't suppose there's any point, but do you remember what we said on our wedding day? Just give me some kind of sign that we can have that again and I'll be on the next plane to Denver.

Number ten.

You can't possibly understand how much this hurts, Joely, when you don't call, you don't take my calls, you don't answer my letters. But I'm not signing the divorce papers. If you want a split, you'll have to talk to me face-to-face. No other options.

Eleven and twelve went right onto the stack. He didn't even bother opening them. Joely's eyes were swimming by now. She swallowed lurking tears, then asked, "Don't I want to hear anything out of those?"

"Nope. I think you get the point." He picked up the pile of letters, carried them to the stove and tossed them in. The fire curled under the sheets of paper, blackening the edges. Eradicating another piece of their past. It felt like surgery. Cauterization. He closed the heavy, wrought iron door and the flames took the letters silently, with no witnesses. Better that way, he was certain.

Presently she said quietly, "So why did you finally come?"

"I took a really close look at those divorce papers and realized I'd been operating on a false assumption."

"That was it?"

He shrugged. "Mostly. Does it really matter, now that I'm here?"

She crossed her arms, staring at the squat, silent stove. "No, I guess it doesn't."

. . .

So they had moved forward, through some of the issues, seeking closure. Joely couldn't help but wonder why she didn't feel any better about it all.

The camaraderie they'd shared through the morning was all but gone. She couldn't look at Rey without thinking about the months before she'd left, when he'd barely spoken to her, and the minutes before she'd left, when she'd said far too much.

The process didn't seem to have affected Rey as deeply, though. He sat watching a cable news channel—after he'd gone outside to scrape the snow off the satellite dish—and seemed not to be agonizing over anything at all. It was a man thing, she supposed, that ability to shrug off a deeply emotional situation and just move on.

Or was it? If he could really shrug things off so easily, what had been the point of his reading the letters? If he could shrug off the pain, he never would have written them in the first place.

Unable to concentrate anymore on the sketches, she found herself looking at the empty shoebox. Finally, she picked it up, took off the lid. There was nothing left inside. She wasn't sure what she'd thought she might find.

"I don't think it was the greatest idea."

She jumped at the sound of Rey's voice and looked up. He was watching her, frowning. He looked sad.

"You think we should have left well enough alone?" she asked.

"Quite likely."

She put the lid back on the box. "It seemed like a good idea at the time. Isn't that the kind of thing a therapist might tell you to do?"

"How the hell should I know? I'm a lawyer." His eyes narrowed as he studied her. The perusal, detached and non-sexual as it was, made her warm. "Let's try something else."

"I'm game."

"Good. The letters have been burned and obliterated—let's say right now that everything associated with them has been, too. All that baggage, all that ugly past. We're starting all fresh. Like—" He paused, then pointed out the window. "Like out there. All the imperfections of the world made right by a layer of snow. Everything smooth and pure and even."

The image appealed to her. "Square one?"

"Square one."

"Which means?"

"That I intend to romance you like you've never been romanced before. You were worth pursuing the first time—I'm sure you're equally worth pursuing again."

She smiled. It actually didn't sound like a bad idea. "Then I look forward to being pursued."

• • •

Well. Now he was going to have to follow through. Like most ideas, it had seemed like a good one at the time. But how was he supposed to romance her in this tiny house, where they couldn't get more than a few yards from each other? Plus, he was at a disadvantage since it was unfamiliar territory.

He considered waiting until tomorrow. Joely had assured him they'd be able to get out of the house in the morning. If he waited, he'd have more resources available to him. But he also would have missed out on his first opportunity to date his wife.

His wife. He hadn't thought about her that way in a long time. His ex-wife, yes, until he'd found out he wasn't really divorced or even close to it. Then he'd come up with several rather uncharitable epithets, until he'd finally just started thinking of her as Joely again. Right now, he felt much as he had during their early courtship. She was a beautiful woman. He sensed a connection that made his body hard and wanting. But he wasn't sure he knew her yet, certainly not as well as he wanted to.

She had disappeared into her bedroom about fifteen minutes ago. Stymied in his romantic pursuits, he decided to check on her.

Peeking around her door, he found her sitting at a small desk looking at spreadsheets on her computer. From what he saw, the data looked good. He watched for a moment while she frowned at the screen, adjusted a few numbers, changed them back, muttered to herself, then combed her fingers through her hair in what looked like frustration. He didn't think it was, though. Just absorption, more likely, a thought-gathering gesture. He took a step forward, not quite into the bedroom, then paused, hearing the rumbling of a vehicle outside.

Joely turned at the sound. Seeing Rey, she lifted her eyebrows questioningly.

"Is that your snowplow?" he asked.

"Sounds like it."

"I'll go check things out."

"I don't think that's really necessary."

Rey shrugged. "Never know. He might need some help."

She grinned, obviously unable to imagine what he could possibly do to help Joe or Roy or Rob or whatever his name was plow the driveway. She was probably right, but he was going, anyway. He wanted to check out this strapping Colorado snowplow guy. See what the competition looked like, if he was competition at all.

He dug his coat out of his suitcase and pulled it on. Unfortunately, he didn't have any boots, so he'd just have to tough it out. He went out to the deck to retrieve the snow shovel he'd used to dig his way to the satellite dish on the side of the house, then went back through the house and out the front door.

Rob the snowplow man proved to be about sixty years old and thus out of the running, but very efficient with the plow.

Rey managed to clear the short sidewalk before Rob finished the driveway, but only barely.

Waving goodbye to Rob, Rey took a moment to take in his surroundings. Snow. Lots of snow. Massive, phenomenal quantities of snow. He was almost certain he'd never seen this much snow, except maybe that one time he and his family had gotten stranded in Buffalo on the way back from a trip to Canada.

A thought came to him. He grinned, blew a long plume of white with his own breath, and set to work.

• • •

Finally done experimenting with permutations and projections, Joely turned off the computer. It occurred to her then that the snowplow had departed quite some time ago, but she hadn't heard Rey come back into the house. Surely he hadn't gotten lost, or frozen to death. Not in less than an hour.

Then again, he was from New York.

She should probably go check on him, just in case. She pulled her coat out of the front closet and opened the front door…

And stopped cold on the front step.

"Hey, Joely!" Rey called.

Laughing, Joely zipped up her coat. "Rey, you're insane."

He only chuckled and went back to work.

He was building a snow fort, the second of two. They were spaced about six yards apart and stood about three feet high at the front. He rolled the last snowball into place to finish off a side wall and straightened. He rubbed his hands together briskly.

"Wanna go at it?" he said.

She did want to go at it. Not in the snow, though. Preferably in a nice, warm bed. Forcing her mind back to what Rey had really meant, Joely stepped off the sidewalk, trudging through the snow to the nearest fort. "Where's the ammunition?"

Rey looked at his watch. "Fifteen minutes to make all you can, then we start."

She jumped the last few steps to the fort and started grabbing handfuls of snow, smashing them into tight, icy snowballs. "You're gonna regret this!" she shouted, and was answered by Rey's laughter.

She thought fifteen minutes would give her plenty of time, but when Rey shouted, "Now!" she looked at her pile of snowballs and its smallness distressed her. Imagining a huge pile of ammunition inside Rey's fort, she shouted back, "Five more minutes!"

"No way!"

She peeked over the front wall of her fort and a snowball flew right at her face. Squeaking in alarm and delight, she ducked and watched it slam into the tree behind her.

"You're dead meat, Rey! You hear me?"

"How could I not?"

She grabbed a handful of the icy snowballs she'd hurriedly smashed together and flung them indiscriminately over the fort wall, not even looking to aim.

"Ow!" said Rey. "You're in for it now!"

The snowballs flew crazily for several frenzied minutes. She screeched and he hollered, she laughed and he let out great howls of mirth. She barely missed his head; he came within inches of hitting her square in the face with a slushy projectile. Finally, emboldened by laughter and adrenaline, she slipped out from behind her fort, then darted across the snow to sneak behind his fort and dump her last three snowballs down the back of his shirt.

He howled in protest and grabbed her, pinning her arms behind her. "I don't even have a decent coat and you do that to me?"

Immobilized against his strong chest, she could do nothing but look up into his laughing face. "I'm sorry."

"No, you're not."

"You're right, I'm not."

"Then neither am I," he said, and kissed her.

His lips were icy cold but the inside of his mouth was warm, his tongue hot as it stroked against her lips. She opened to him, pressing hard into his heat. Snow and cold forgotten, she sought only that warmth, that union. His mouth on hers, soft and mobile, his tongue pressing softly against hers. He pulled her close, his hands sliding down her back.

She clutched at his coat, so absorbed it was a few long seconds before she registered the cold, the wet. As she pulled back, he ducked forward, his mouth still seeking hers even as she ended the kiss.

"You're soaked," she said. "We should get you inside."

He dipped his head one more time toward her, and when he missed, he smiled a little and said, "Yeah. My shoes are full of snow and my jeans are soaked."

"You're going to catch pneumonia." Fighting the reluctance of her entire body, she took a step back. Her hand sought his, unwilling to break the connection totally. "Come on. I'll make you some hot cocoa."

•••

So here she was, taking care of him again. It had been unsettling the first time but he was starting to get used to it.

She'd led him into the house by the hand, as if he were a little boy, or a newly discovered beau. He preferred the latter. The simple act of holding her hand felt so profound right now. The kiss had been better, but perhaps it had been too much to expect right now.

"Get into some dry clothes," she suggested. She closed the door behind them and grasped his coat by the collar, helping him out of it. He kicked off his cold, soggy tennis shoes and padded in wet socks into the living room. Pausing by the fire, he held his hands out. The heat felt good on cold, stiff fingers. He stood there for a few seconds, letting his joints loosen in the warmth before he started to unbutton his shirt.

"Think you could help me out of the rest of this?" He hazarded a look back toward the kitchen, where Joely was stirring cocoa powder into mugs of milk.

She gave him an arch look. "I think you can manage to undress yourself."

"I don't know. It's harder to get stuff off when it's wet."

"Don't push it, Rey."

She didn't sound nearly as irritated as she could have. He smiled and yanked at his jeans. The wet denim was heavy and tried to cling to his skin. It really would have been easier with Joely pulling on the cuffs. But she was right. He was capable of undressing himself. He was also capable of doing it right in the middle of the living room, where she couldn't miss it.

He was down to his underwear—also wet, and clinging like cellophane to all his manly bits—when she came in with the mugs of cocoa.

"Did you want some privacy?" she asked, looking directly into his eyes.

"Why?" He took a mug from her hand. "There's nothing here you haven't seen before. Hell, you've had your hands—not to mention your mouth—all over everything I've got. What's the big deal?"

She blushed and turned away, but not before her gaze flicked downward for a split second. She swallowed and looked back up, and he felt momentarily repentant for flaunting himself at her. But only momentarily. "I haven't agreed to this thing about you being my husband again," she informed him. "And I think you standing naked in my living room is a little more husband-like than I'm ready for at the moment."

The corner of his mouth quirked up. "I'm not naked."

"Close enough." Setting her cocoa on the end table, she stuck her hand in his suitcase and produced a pair of briefs. "Here. These are dry."

She threw them at him. He caught them. "Thanks." But when he set down his own cocoa and started to peel off the wet underwear, she turned her back on him and walked back into the kitchen.

He shook his head, disappointed. *Oh, well. One step at a time.*

He pulled on his jeans and went to see what she had found to do in the kitchen. But she wasn't doing anything—just standing looking out the window, into the snow-filled side yard. He stepped up behind her, almost close enough for his bare chest to touch her back, but not quite.

She turned her head slightly toward him, just enough to acknowledge his presence but not far enough to look at him.

"That was fun," she said.

He nodded. Her shoulders shifted just a little, as if inviting his touch. Hoping he was reading her signals right, he eased an inch or so closer and settled his arms around her waist. She settled back into him. He closed his eyes and let his cheek fall against her head, breathing the smell of her hair. So sweet, so full of memories, just that flowery shampoo smell almost brought tears to his eyes.

"What made you think of it?" she went on.

He was so surprised and gratified by her acceptance he almost missed the question. Opening his eyes brought him back to reality, where he could concentrate. "I was going to build something romantic. I don't know, a giant snow-heart, or a couple of snowmen holding hands."

"Why didn't you?"

"Apparently I lack snow-sculpturing ability. My fort was the beginning of the heart, plus what was left after the first snowman fell down. Then once I had one fort it seemed like I should build another one."

She laughed. "How untalented do you have to be to lack snow-sculpturing ability?"

He chuckled against her hair, unoffended. "It's one of those balance things, I think. You possess unlimited sculpturing ability in all forms, therefore I'm not allowed to have any ability in any form."

She turned around to face him. Her hands curled against his bare chest as she looked up into his eyes. "Yeah, but *snow*?"

"What can I say?"

Her lips seemed to beckon him with the curve of their smile. He wanted so much to kiss her here in the warm kitchen, to relive the moment they'd shared outside in the snow. But he didn't dare. Not just yet.

Later. Later, he promised himself, he would do more than kiss her. He would cup her breasts in his hands and kiss them, let his fingers remember every soft, warm inch of her skin. He would find all the beauty he remembered in the heat of her body's most secret places. And never again would he forget the preciousness of those moments.

Right now, though, he just looked into the depths of her blue eyes. "We used to have a lot of fun together."

It was a risk, he knew, and when her smile turned sad, he began to wish he hadn't taken it. "Yes, we did." She shifted back a bit, partially breaking the contact between them. When she spoke again, her voice had gone edgy. "It's all fun and games until somebody gets their heart broken."

She slid away from him, out of his half embrace, and retreated to the living room. He took a long breath, her departure dropping a weight onto his formerly buoyant heart.

One step at a time. Should he go after her? He wasn't sure. He wanted to, but something made him think he should err on the side of caution this time. He opened the refrigerator instead.

...

The problem with this house, Joely thought, was that it just wasn't big enough. Sure, there was enough room for her furniture, and some books and clothes, but not even close to enough room for six feet of pheromone-producing male.

She sat on the couch and pulled her knees to her chest, making herself as small as she could. Defenses in place, she peered into the kitchen.

He was rummaging through the refrigerator, apparently looking for sandwich ingredients. The muscles in his wide, bare back moved and rippled under his skin. Just the shape of his shoulder blades aroused her. She chewed on a fingernail.

She had two choices. She could fight this tooth and nail, out of fear, or she could take a leap of faith and see where it took her. Which was the right choice? She honestly had no idea. And it was so hard to think when he was in there flaunting his beautifully constructed chest.

One thing she knew for certain—he was spending another night on the couch. Even that wasn't quite far enough. She felt like she needed some distance, so she could make a rational decision.

Was there such a thing as a rational decision in this situation? She wasn't even sure about that. This wasn't a business decision— it was a matter of the heart.

Unfortunately, she wasn't at all sure she could trust hers anymore.

Chapter Six

The next morning, she found him shivering again in the kitchen, pouring freshly brewed coffee into a mug. At least he was dressed this time. "Good morning," he said when he saw her. "Want some?" He gestured toward the coffee.

"Sure. Thanks." She went to the table and sat. This was nice, actually. Nice to be waited on for a change.

She watched him pour the coffee, then he sat across from her at the table, pushing her cup toward her. He curled his hands around his mug, letting the steam caress his face. He was still shivering.

"Cold?" she asked.

He shuddered. "You really should turn up the heat a little."

"You really should wear some pajamas to bed."

He made a face. "Pajamas are for wimps."

"I wear them."

"You're a girl."

"I see." She smiled and sipped her coffee, watching him desperately clutch the heat of his mug. "I'm not shivering, though."

"All you have to do is turn the heat up."

"Heat's for wimps."

His eyebrow quirked, his mouth compressing as if holding back a smile. "Touché." He swigged down the last of his coffee and went back for more.

She watched his retreat into the kitchen, focusing on the way his jeans hugged his rear end. Maybe she wouldn't have to worry about his staying the whole month. His citified, pretty-boy genes couldn't take it in the mountains.

"It'd be a lot warmer if we'd been in bed together," he said then, and she rolled her eyes reflexively as he leered and poured more coffee.

"We'd just be that much colder now. It's like getting out of the hot tub when it's snowing outside. It feels twenty degrees colder because you're already so warm."

His eyebrows rose. "You have a hot tub?"

"Yes, I do."

His sober nod spelled danger. Something was going on behind those gray eyes. He was hatching some kind of plan. "Sounds nice," was all he said.

She decided to let that rest, for fear of putting other thoughts into his head. Let him work out his seduction scenario on his own. "I have to be at work in a half hour. What do you want to do?"

He gave her a wicked grin. "What do you mean by that?"

"You know what I mean." She barely repressed the urge to roll her eyes. "You can come with me, or stay here and try to drive down to the shop later. I can leave you directions." Rey had never been much for driving, though, city boy that he was. She was half afraid he might end up in Shawnee if he tried to drive to the shop by himself. Or Utah.

"I'll come with you."

"Are you sure? It might be just as dull at the shop."

"Maybe, but there are other places within walking distance of the shop. I can snoop around what passes for downtown if I get tired of hanging out with the pots and jewelry. Plus I can follow you in my rental car, so if I get too bored I can come back here or take a drive or something."

"That's fine." She stood, drained her coffee mug and set it in the sink. "I'll be ready in a bit."

He wanted to follow her into the bathroom and watch her morning routine. He'd always enjoyed watching her put on her makeup. He liked the funny faces she made when she applied her mascara. But he had some things to get ready, too. He finished his coffee and toast, found eggs in the refrigerator and started a couple frying on the stove, then headed into the living room. His laptop was ready to go, already folded up in its case. He checked the outside pocket of the case for his digital camera. His USB drive was in another pocket, and he also had power cables for the computer. All set. With luck, he could get some work done while he was out, provided he could stay under Joely's radar.

The eggs were just the right side of done when Joely emerged from the bathroom, her porcelain skin even lovelier under a light application of cosmetics. He took a moment to absorb the sight of her, then turned back to his eggs.

"We have to go," she told him, coming into the kitchen with her giant purse slung over her shoulder. "You don't have time to eat those."

"No problem." He snagged two more pieces of bread from the loaf and dumped the eggs out of the skillet between them, making a sandwich. "I'm ready."

She smiled a little, and he was encouraged to see the softness in it. "I forgot you need more than toast in the morning."

"I'm a big, strapping man. I need protein."

She laughed. He grinned and followed her out the door.

• • •

From behind the counter, Joely and Perry watched Rey as he studied the merchandise in the front jewelry cabinet. He was squatting on the floor in front of the case, and the position did such marvelous things to his thighs and buttocks that it was hard for Joely to concentrate on Perry's earnest advice.

"Don't stand there drooling at him and ignoring me and tell me you don't still love him," Perry finally said, in half-mock exasperation.

"Lusting after him and loving him aren't the same thing."

"I'm sorry, hon, but that's not lust." Joely looked at her in surprise. Perry shook her head with a tolerant smile. "There's something in your eyes I've never seen before."

"Really? What?"

Perry nodded sagely. "Fear. And lust, my dear, does not inspire fear."

Rey straightened and turned toward the shop's high, wide back window, giving the women a view of his clean profile.

"Look at him," Joely muttered. "He's not even that good-looking. I mean, look at his nose. It's huge."

"Is he in proportion?" Perry's eyes twinkled lewdly.

Thinking about the wet cotton briefs and what they had failed miserably to conceal, Joely nodded. "More or less." She sighed again, then shook her head. "I can't throw him out. Not now. There's too much—" She broke off, unwilling to face the emotion her words had begun to evoke. "I have to give it a chance." Rey stepped closer to the window, and Joely looked at Perry. "Do you think it's the right thing to do?"

"I think if it weren't, you wouldn't be agonizing over it so much."

"You might be right about that." She crossed her arms firmly over her chest. Just then, Rey turned his head to look at her and smile. She smiled back, but she knew it looked forced, and her brow refused to unbeetle.

But her soberness only made his smile widen. He knew, she thought. Somehow, he knew exactly what she'd been thinking, and he knew what decision she'd made.

Well, good for him. That would save her having to actually tell him. Inexplicably angry, she wheeled and huffed into the office, slamming the door behind her.

• • •

Rey couldn't help laughing a little at Joely's vehement departure. He hadn't been able to hear what she and Perry had been saying, but he'd known damn well they were talking about him. Joely was, he knew, agonizing over what could have been a simple decision. Keep him or kick him out. Yes or no. Why did it have to be so hard?

He wasn't being fair, though. He'd come out of nowhere, asking more than he should have. If he hadn't been so desperate to get her back, he never would have forced himself on her like this. But living without her had been like living without part of his heart. He needed her back, and it was hard for him to imagine she might not feel the same way.

In any case, it looked like she'd made her decision. He was going to get his probation period. The next question was, how far to push it? Did he dare imagine he might be able to get her into bed tonight? The thought made him weak inside. It had been nearly eighteen months since the last time they'd made love—his fault, for ignoring her those months before she'd finally packed up and left. And he hadn't touched another woman since the last time he'd touched Joely. His body hurt with his need for her. It was all he could do to keep standing there, nonchalant, smiling now at Perry, then returning his attention to the gorgeous sweep of scenery out the wide window.

"It's pretty up here," he said, nodding toward the window, surprised his voice sounded normal rather than strangled and tortured.

"Yes, it is," Perry said. Something tight in her tone made him look at her. She had her arms crossed over her chest and was regarding him with one eyebrow cocked. "If you hurt her," she said, "I'll kill you."

Rey's smile fell off his face. He'd thought Perry was on his side. "I—" he started, then faltered under the intensity of Perry's glare.

The bell on the front door rang and a young woman came in, a little girl balanced on her hip. Perry cast Rey one last dark look. "I mean it, Rey."

Rey swallowed. "I believe you."

"Good."

Perry turned to her new customer then, her face changing from deathly threat to smiles and charm. Rey, disconcerted, shook his head.

Between the unpredictable weather and the unpredictable women, Colorado was a scary place.

Chapter Seven

Joely left at eleven-thirty for lunch. Rey took advantage of her absence to slip into the office.

"Just want to check my e-mail," he told Perry, who gave him a dubious nod.

He wasn't lying—he *did* want to check his e-mail. He pulled out his computer and booted it up.

Putting Joely completely out of his mind, he glanced over the half-dozen messages he'd received since yesterday. Officially, he was on vacation, but his boss, Bill, knew what he was up to and had sent several notes regarding the case they were building together. Rey still hadn't gotten pictures of Joely's pots, but that shouldn't be too difficult if they continued to give him free access to the shop. He dropped Bill a note to that effect, filing the other messages for later reference.

He was just about to shut the computer off when Perry stuck her head in.

"Hey, do you think you could watch the place for about five minutes while I use the bathroom?" she said.

Perfect. "Not a problem. I'll be there in a sec."

"Great." She let the door fall shut behind her. He snagged his digital camera out of the pocket of his computer case and slid it into his pants pocket. It was a tiny, slim little thing, perfect for this kind of work.

When he came out of the office, Perry nodded her thanks and scooted off to the bathroom. By the time she got back, Rey had taken twenty-five pictures of Joely's assortment of clay pots, in addition to helping four customers.

"Thanks," said Perry.

"Not a problem." He went back into the office, hooked his camera into his computer, and e-mailed the pictures to Bill with a note: "Look at Cherokee's new lineup. Check for wolves."

• • •

Joely stood in the tiny general store next to the gas station across the street from her shop. She hadn't even known, until five minutes ago, that they carried any form of birth control.

Since she'd been too embarrassed to ask anyone where to look, it had taken her ten minutes of wandering around the little store before she managed to find the small selection of condoms. Now she just stood there staring at them, looking, she assumed, like a complete idiot, trying to work up the nerve to buy some.

She had to, though. There were some things she just wasn't willing to risk, not even to have Rey back in her life. Pregnancy was one of them. She wasn't really worried about anything else, not with Rey, but she definitely didn't want any of his strapping, healthy man-sperm to make her life any more of a debacle than it already was.

Finally, she just grabbed a box and shoved it under her arm. It occurred to her that might make it look like she was shoplifting. So she shifted it so it was barely visible and headed for the counter.

At the last minute, she realized she should have bought something else, too. Buying just a box of condoms was so—well, it made it look like she thought she was going to be having sex tonight. If she'd bought some other things, like milk or ice cream, maybe the condoms would have looked like an afterthought.

It was too late. She was standing in front of the counter with her box of condoms, and she'd look even crazier if she turned around and ran. So she set the box down, feeling her face go hot.

"Hi, Ms. Birch," said the girl behind the counter, and Joely suddenly recognized her as a high school girl who'd worked for her for a few weeks during the summer. Could this get any more humiliating?

"Hi, Darla," Joely mumbled.

"I hear your husband's in town," said Darla brightly, then looked down at Joely's single item. Her lips clamped shut and she, too, blushed. In silence, she rung up the condoms and took Joely's cash. Joely grabbed the box and ran, not even waiting for Darla to put it in a bag.

After all this, I damn well better get some, and it better be good.

• • •

With pictures sent and mission accomplished, at least for the moment, Rey decided to spend the rest of the afternoon away from the shop. It was getting hard for him to be in such close proximity to Joely, thinking about what might or might not happen tonight. In addition, business began to pick up right after she came back from lunch at twelve-fifteen, and he was beginning to feel like he was in the way.

Joely barely looked at him as he headed out the door. She looked like her lunch had been traumatic, and he wondered what could have happened. Maybe she'd tell him later. Or maybe she wouldn't. The thought bothered him. Once upon a time, they'd told each other everything.

He shoved his regrets aside. The more he thought about the past, the more he was reminded that his current situation was mostly his own fault, and that didn't help him focus on his purpose. He had to concentrate on the present, so the future would fall into place. He couldn't do anything about the past, so there was no point brooding about it. Besides, if everything went the way he planned, he'd make amends for much of what had driven him and Joely apart.

Right now, he needed to think about tonight. He was almost positive Joely was going to accept his proposal rather than throw him out of her house. This was a good thing. But he had to make sure it was going to work. He needed a plan.

Standing on the sidewalk in front of Joely's shop, he surveyed his surroundings, assessing his resources. There was a little country store that looked like it stocked basic necessities, a card and gift shop, a liquor store, a florist, the diner, and, a short way up the road, the lodge where he'd stayed his first night here. He smiled as bits of ideas started to bump together in his head. This could work. This could, in fact, work extremely well.

• • •

Two hours later, he stood in front of the desk at the Sky Mountain Lodge, ringing the bell. Several large paper and plastic bags sat on the floor next to his feet. Appearing from behind a door leading to a back room, Virginia tilted him a smile.

"Mr. Birch, right?" she said.

"You know damn well it's Mr. Birch," he answered with a grin. "You never did explain why you threw me out."

She grinned back at him. "You didn't put your towels away."

"I most certainly did."

Still grinning, Virginia pointed at a sign on the wall. "'Management reserves the right to refuse service to anyone for any reason,'" she read.

"Even spurious reasons?"

"That is correct, Mr. Birch." She had a definite twinkle in her eye. Rey leaned into the counter, matching that mischievous gaze with a conniving look of his own.

"I have a theory, Virginia," he said.

"And what would that be?"

"I think you threw me out of the lodge because you wanted me to end up in bed with Joely."

Her eyes narrowed, but she was still smiling. "Go on."

"It didn't work. I ended up on her couch, and my back's still paying for it." He straightened his spine, which responded with an obliging crack. Virginia winced. "Anyway, I'm thinking that since this was your plan, and since it didn't work the way it was supposed to, you might be willing to help me with my personal plan, which, in deference to you, I'll refer to as 'Phase Two.'"

She studied him reflectively. "You know, you could have charmed the pants right off me back in the day."

"I'll take that as a compliment."

"As well you should. I was quite the catch."

"I'm sure you still are. So what do you think? Are you in?"

Her lips pursed as she considered. "You're right, you know, about why I kicked you out."

He nodded, trying not to look smug.

"But I'm not sure, now, it was the right thing to do."

"Why not?"

"Because I was sticking my nose where it didn't belong." She crossed her arms over her chest. "If I helped you out, I'd be doing exactly that again."

He offered his most charming smile. "Has that ever stopped you before?"

"You've got a point there." She uncrossed her arms, dropping her fists on her hips. "What do you need?"

"I just need directions to Joely's."

She gave him a long, hard look. Then she pulled a piece of paper and a pen out from under the counter and started writing.

• • •

Joely was carefully wrapping a ceramic owl in tissue paper when the phone rang. Perry picked it up, talked for a moment, then gave Joely a flirty look as she hung up.

"That was Rey," she said.

Joely eased the well-cushioned owl into a gift box. "What did he want?"

"Nothing. He just said not to worry about him. He got directions from Virginia and drove up to your place about an hour ago."

"Did you want this gift-wrapped?" Joely asked the customer, then her confusion kicked in. "He did what?"

The customer, a young woman in an extremely pink blouse, said, "No, no gift wrap. Who's Rey?"

"Her husband," said Perry, and Joely said, "My ex."

The woman smiled. "That's what I love about this place. It's always so interesting." She picked up her carefully packaged owl and departed, grinning.

Joely shrugged, trying not to let her imagination get away with her. "Maybe he just got bored."

"Maybe he's waiting on your couch. Naked." She gave a cheeky grin. "You know, with that big nose and everything."

Joely scowled. "Don't start, Perry."

"I'd hurry home if I were you."

"We close in an hour. I'll go home then."

She spent the next hour pretending she had no concerns at all about what Rey might be doing alone in her house. But by the time she turned over the "Closed" sign, her stomach was trembling with anticipation. He'd said he was going to seduce her, and she had reason to know he could do a fine job of it, if he set his mind to it. She pulled out the cash drawer, preparing to take it back to the office to lock it in the safe, but Perry grabbed it.

"I'll take care of this stuff. You go home and see what's up."

Joely opened her mouth to protest, then realized she didn't want to. "Okay. Thanks, Perry. Don't count it. We can do that in the morning. I'll come in early."

"Somehow I doubt that," said Perry.

Joely gave her a tolerant smile and a half-amused roll of the eyes. But, secretly, she thought maybe Perry was right.

•••

Rubbing his hands together, Rey perused his work. The table was set with some pretty stoneware he'd found in Joely's cabinets. It didn't look familiar; she must have bought it after she'd moved. Or maybe she'd made it. It didn't have her mark on the bottom, but the pattern looked like something she'd come up with, with its vibrant, offbeat colors and not-quite symmetrical pattern. In the middle of the table was a large bouquet flanked by candles, which he'd lit. The lady at the florist shop had said they had aromatherapy oils in them that would increase the romantic mood. Rey wasn't sure he believed in aromatherapy, but he needed all the help he could get. So there were six more candles in the kitchen, burning in different places, adding atmosphere and a subtle fragrance Rey hoped would work its magic on Joely.

He wondered if it would work, though, if the aromatherapy smell was drowned out by the dinner smell. He'd bought dinner to go at the diner and had it warming now in the oven. Virginia had given him suggestions on the diner's specialties after she'd written up the directions to Joely's house. So, at the moment, the smell of the candles was barely discernible beneath the smell of warming buffalo burritos. Whatever those were. He hoped they were good.

He'd prepared the bedroom, too, hoping to end up there at some point. There were more candles in there, more flowers, a bottle of champagne. As far as he knew, everything was ready for a full-charge, take-no-prisoners seduction.

Okay, maybe the wartime metaphors weren't the best. But he was a guy—it was the best he could do.

The sound of gravel crunching in the long driveway was the signal he'd been waiting for. He pulled the wine bottle out of the fridge and set it on the table, then settled himself on the couch, legs crossed. No, legs uncrossed. No, crossed. One arm over the back of the sofa? Maybe he should take off his clothes…No, that was pushing it. No point looking like a *Playgirl* spread. Nonchalant sitting should do it.

Crossed. No, uncrossed.

Too late. Joely opened the door and walked in. She stopped and stared. At him, at the candles, at the bottle of wine on the table.

"What's all this?" she asked.

"Dinner."

She nodded, slowly and dubiously. "I see." Looking more closely at him, she said, "You look nice."

"Thanks." He hadn't been sure what to wear, so he'd settled on jeans, because when he wore them, she kept staring at his ass, and a casual cotton shirt that buttoned down the front, because it would be easy to get out of when the time came. Apparently, they went well together. He was glad Joely approved.

Joely took off her jacket and hung it and her purse on the coat tree by the door. "So, what's cooking?"

"Buffalo burritos and some rice and beans from the diner." He turned as she walked into the kitchen and opened the oven to look in.

"Sounds good," she said.

"I wasn't sure about the burritos, but Virginia recommended them. Are they like buffalo wings, or what?"

Joely gave him an odd look. "No, Rey, it's buffalo meat. You know, buffalo? Those big hairy cows?" She wiggled her index fingers next to her temples, imitating small, curled bison horns.

"Oh." There was a stupid city-boy mistake if there ever was one. "Is that kind of like thinking Rocky Mountain Oysters are really oysters?"

She laughed. "Not quite that bad."

Her warm smile made him feel less stupid. He got up and followed her into the kitchen. "So, are you hungry?"

"Yes, I am—"

She turned to face him and he caught her, first with his arms, then with his mouth against hers. For a moment she held herself stiff against him, then she melted, slowly but thoroughly.

The barriers were coming down. He could feel them falling one by one as she pressed harder into him, her mouth opening under his. Right now, if he let his hands slide forward to mound her breasts against his palms, he knew she wouldn't pull away. But he didn't do it. He walked his fingers softly down her back, just to where her waist met her hips, dancing along the beginnings of that rounded rise. No farther.

He wanted her. More than he could allow himself to show right now. Wanted to taste her skin, her mouth, her body, wanted to bury himself in her, possess her as he had so many times before. Wanted to remind her who she belonged to. But he couldn't rush her, not right now. He knew she was going to say yes, albeit later, so there was no need. He flattened his hands against her waist and tucked her a little closer against him while his tongue reacquainted itself with the taste of her mouth. Long, slow, gentle strokes, more than chaste, not quite lustful.

She whimpered and her fingers dug hard into his shoulders. Slowly, he drew back. Arousal pounded through his body, making him crazy, making him want more than he should try to take right now. One step at a time, let her lead the way, but his body wanted so much more. His mind, his heart, wanted to be part of her again. He shifted his position against her. He was hard and getting harder, and he didn't want to prod her. Didn't want to make her think he was forcing the issue.

"We should eat," he said.

Her eyes staring into his had gone dark and glassy with need. She blinked up at him, comprehension slowly returning to her face.

"Yes," she finally said, in a weak voice. "That would be a good idea."

•••

Joely picked at her dinner. She couldn't bring herself to eat more than half of one of the heavy, cheese-drenched burritos. The rice was lighter and didn't land in her stomach like a rock, but even that lost its appeal after a few forkfuls.

She poked at the cheese that had melted across her plate, twirling it around the tines of her fork, then laid the fork down and folded her hands in her lap.

"What's the matter?" Rey asked. He'd demolished an entire burrito and a pile of rice and beans, plus at least two glasses of wine.

"Nothing. It's a lot of food."

"No dessert, then?"

The diner was famous for its pies, but Joely's stomach wouldn't stop fluttering. She was unaccountably nervous, her hands trembling, her breath too fast, her heartbeat pattering in the back of her throat. "Probably not."

"That's okay. It'll keep."

He sipped his wine, then set it back down. She watched his hand as it cupped the wineglass, then drew slowly away. His fingers lingered against the rounded belly of the glass and she thought about yesterday, the warmth of his mouth in the cold and snow—

"Rey…" She trailed off, not sure she could say anymore. Still looking at the wineglass, she gathered her courage. "Rey, I want to try it."

He said nothing. Surprised at the silence, she finally looked up, only to find him looking right at her, an undeniable smolder in his eyes.

"The pie?" he said quietly. "Or me?"

She couldn't laugh. She was too scared. "You, Rey. You've got your month."

He laid his hand on the table in front of her, palm up. "Thank you."

For the space of a long breath, she could only stare at his hand, the tapered fingers, the creases across his wide palm. Then, shivering a little, she lifted her own hand and slid it into his. His fingers curled around hers gently.

"I still love you, Joely." His voice seemed to come from far away.

"I know," she said, and squeezed his hand.

• • •

As the dinner smells faded, another, subtler aroma took over. Not quite floral, not quite citrus, it gave Joely a soft, melty feeling. It was the candles, she realized. Rey had obviously talked to all the right people. Tara at the gift shop knew all about aromatherapy.

It touched her that he'd gone to so much trouble. He'd been like this when they'd first started going out—romantic and willing to spare no expense to give her a memorable evening. It had lasted for a year or so into their marriage, even.

They were on the couch by now, the remains of dinner left to itself. Joely couldn't even muster enough interest to scrape the plates or put the leftovers in the fridge, not with Rey looking at her with sex smoldering in his eyes, and the smell from the candles growing stronger. She leaned into him, fisting his shirt in her hand. Her tongue traced his lips, remembering the shape. His lower lip was full and pillowy, the upper thin but bowed, the combined effect one of irresistible sensuality. He knew how to use that mouth, too. She wanted him to use it tonight in as many ways as he could think of.

He cupped her elbow in one hand, but made no further overtures as she slowly undid his shirt buttons. She slid her hands inside, drawing her fingers through the rough hair, finding his nipples and rubbing them with her thumbs until they rose under her encouragement. He drew in a quick breath and let it out, and his fingers tightened a little on her elbow.

"Touch me," she whispered. He was waiting for her permission, she was certain, giving her control. At her words, he sighed and scooped his hands under the tail of her shirt. His palms slid up her back to the clasp of her bra and worried it open. Then his hands moved forward, until her breasts settled into the curve of his fingers.

She leaned harder into him, pressing her breasts into his hands. Her nipples strained against his palms, tingling with arousal that shot through her body, pooling in taut heat between her legs. She wanted him so badly, it was like insanity pulsing through her blood. Wanted to possess him, wanted him to possess her. She remembered what it was like to have him inside her—he could fill her hard and deep, and he knew how to make her scream. But she was afraid. She felt like a virgin. He'd been inside her more times than she could count, but right now it was as if she had never made love to him at all.

He kissed her again, his mouth hard and insistent. No more polite waiting. His tongue moved in an urgent rhythm, hot in her mouth, his hands stoking the flame. Need stabbed through her body as he rolled her nipples between thumb and forefinger, squeezed and teased them. The clothes had to go—no question about that. Writhing into the movement of his hands, she worked her way out of her shirt, her bra, peeling his shirt off him as well, until finally she could press bare skin against bare skin. She drew a harsh breath, overwhelmed the sensation. It had been so long…

Not too late to turn back. You don't have to go through with it. But of course she did. She wanted it too much. His warm skin, the rough texture of the hair on his chest, rubbing against her nipples. His heartbeat against her, the rhythm of his breathing. She remembered a day when she had craved him, times she would have sold her own soul just to touch him. Days she thought she might die if she couldn't have him inside her.

This was one of those days.

His fingers found the buttons at her waistband, loosened them, then trailed down her thighs, her calves, as he slid her pants off her. She closed her eyes. Gentle, careful fingers, barely brushing her skin, creating new lines of fire through her body. Eager, greedy, she pulled at his jeans until they slid undone down his hips. She hesitated, surprised at her own uncertainty. She had made love to this man a hundred times—more. Why did it feel so different this time? As if she no longer knew how to touch him?

She took a breath, trying to allay the thin shiver of apprehension, and put her hand against the straining cotton of his briefs. He moaned. That was good. She remembered that sound. It meant she'd done something right. She smiled.

Confidence beginning to return, she peeled off the briefs, her hand conforming to the familiar curve of his ass. His skin twitched a little under her touch, and she felt goose bumps rise. The muscle there was still firm and round, still very grabbable, making her think he hadn't stopped his regular workout. Her other hand rose to cup the other buttock, and she hesitated before pulling him in toward her, opening her legs, drawing him between them.

It felt right to have him there. Like he belonged. Of course he did. They'd been perfectly matched in so many ways. Sex had always been incendiary between them. Bed-rattlingly hot. Her skin lit up, anticipating reunion, re-acquaintance, the oh-so-familiar, oh-so-achingly, suddenly new sensation of penetration. Inside her. She needed him inside her.

She traced her fingers forward, to the front curve of his hipbone, then down, touching the springy curls of his hair, finally touching the tips of her fingers to the root of his sex. She couldn't help a smug smile when he flinched. He caressed her hair, bent to kiss her, drawing her head in as he softly devoured her mouth. The taste of wine and salsa still lingered in his mouth, and she pressed her tongue in deep, tasting it all. Her fingers pressed gently against his erection. Memory flooded through her, recalling the exact shape of him, the textures of his skin. She traced his hard length, the slight curve, touching the rim, caressing around it, then gently up the slick skin to the tip.

He pushed her hand away.

"What?" she asked, wondering if she'd been too rough in her enthusiasm.

He smiled a little, crookedly, his fingers curling over hers in a caress. "It's been a long time. I'm going to be way too far ahead of you if you keep that up."

Freeing her fingers from his, she traced the back of her hand up his belly until her nails brushed his nipples. "How long?"

"As long as it's been for you."

She swallowed a sudden lump of emotion and pressed her face into his chest, kissing the hollow between his pectoral muscles, letting his hair tickle her face. He had waited, too. He had waited.

Drawing her firmly against him, he slipped his hand into her panties, his fingers dipping into her folds. A rush of arousal followed his touch, her body heating up, wetness flooding her. She stilled at the intense sensation. Tears had come to her eyes.

She wasn't sure if they were from regret, happiness, or just arousal. Maybe all of the above.

He stopped, too, fingers still inside her, but withdrawing a little. She shivered.

"It's not too late," he murmured. "You can still tell me no."

She shook her head.

He seemed surprised. "You're sure? You're sure you want this?"

She thought she should answer him aloud, but found herself incapable of forming words. They seemed to be stranded somewhere between her brain and her lips.

Instead she groped between the couch cushions, where she'd hidden a condom. She opened the package and sheathed him. He gasped as her fingers slid down him, unrolling the thin latex.

Pleased by the reaction, she pulled her panties out of the way, not bothering to take them off, just pushing the crotch material to the side. She grasped his shaft and pulled him toward her, then held him there for a moment. The weight of him there, pressing against her sensitive flesh, just on the verge of penetration, made her want to weep with joy. She blinked back another round of unexpected tears.

His hips pulsed, automatically, she thought, and she moved her own hips back to keep him from penetrating her. She wasn't ready. Not yet. Instead, she took firm hold of his shaft and moved him up and down, toying with him, a small distance in, then sliding him out.

He arched his head back, emitting a low, breathy moan. It occurred to her belatedly that she'd never taken charge with him quite in this way. She'd been taking care of him; now she was aggressive with him, controlling the dynamic of the encounter. He didn't seem to mind.

She undulated her hips, stroking him with her body, letting only the barest tip of him inside her. God, it felt good. It was like heaven. Not just because it was sex. Because it was Rey.

He braced his hands against her shoulders, not controlling her movement at all, but meshing with her rhythm, moving with her, as she pressed harder and harder against him.

Finally, her body full of heat and light and something she tentatively wanted to call happiness, she let go of him and moved forward, until he was inside her. He hesitated, but only for a moment, as if waiting for a signal. But she'd already given the signal when she'd let him go. He took a breath, short and shallow, then pushed into her, deep, firm, all the way to the root.

She closed her eyes and smiled. It was just as she'd remembered it, but more. It had been so long that it felt brand new, like something she'd never done before. At the same time, she remembered this sensation, of being taken, claimed, so full of him she could barely contain it. She threw her head back and let out a sound of pleasure mixed with triumph.

He arched over her, pressing her back into the couch, filling her more thoroughly than she would have thought possible, bringing back every memory she owned of them like this, open to and claimed by each other, giving and receiving, filled and filling. Flame spiraled through her as he thrust into her. He withdrew, pushed hard in again, and she dug her fingers deep into his shoulders, just holding onto him. He lost himself to the rhythm, thrusting, possessing her, enthusiastic but not hard, just Rey, deep and solid inside her. Fire built in her body until it rose and exploded, radiating through every inch of her body. Even her fingertips climaxed.

She smiled and cried out, shivering as he clutched at her and thrust again, again, two or five more times, deep enough to strike her womb, sending the sensation reverberating into her chest, until finally he, too, shuddered and gasped his way to completion.

He set his forehead against her shoulder, a fine sheen of sweat covering his sculpted back. "That was supposed to happen in the bedroom," he whispered. "I had the bedroom all ready."

"The candles work too well," she answered, smiling.

He laughed a little and kissed her softly, first on her mouth, then on the tip of her nose. He was still inside her and she shifted a little, taking him farther in before she lost that connection completely.

"We were always good in bed," he said. "You can't argue with that."

"No," she replied. "No, I really can't."

"I guess we're good on the couch, too." Laughing a little, he maneuvered his way off the couch and scooped his arms under her. "Let's take this someplace more comfortable."

• • •

The cuddling was almost as good as the sex. She lay spooned against his stomach in her almost too-small bed, sipping from the glass of champagne he'd poured for her, smelling the candles burning on the chest of drawers. There were flowers there, too—a large bouquet of carnations and daisies. It was all so perfect.

Too perfect, even. A tear gathered at the corner of her eye and she flicked it away, surreptitiously she thought. But Rey, curled behind her, laid his chin on her shoulder and said, "What's wrong, Joely?"

"Nothing."

"No, there's something. Tell me. Please?"

"This is wonderful," she said, her voice wobbly.

"Yes, it is." She could tell from his tone that he was waiting for her to drop the other shoe.

"But there's more to it than this, isn't there?" More than just the sex, more than the way he could make her burn, more than the way he felt like he belonged inside her body. They'd had that once and had thrown it away—how could they be sure they could find it again?

He tightened his arm around her waist, but gave her no answer.

Chapter Eight

Joely woke at her usual time the next morning, even though she hadn't set the alarm clock. It hadn't been a comfortable night, as there simply wasn't enough room in her bed for two people. Rey didn't seem to have been bothered, though—he lay on his side snoring, one arm dangling off the edge of the bed. If he moved only slightly the wrong way, he'd fall flat on her braided area rug.

She slipped carefully out of the bed, resolutely focusing her attention on the closet, thinking about what she could wear today. If she looked back at the bed, where he still lay sleeping, she wasn't sure she could be responsible for the consequences. She would climb back under the covers, meld herself to his warm body, wake him up, ride him until she screamed…

Not the kind of thoughts that were conducive to getting her to work on time. Forcing them to follow a different track, she closed her hand on the handle of the closet door. *Pink sweater. It's supposed to be chilly today. Maybe a skirt. I haven't worn a skirt in a while.*

She looked.

He had rolled on his back toward the center of the bed, one arm flung across the space she'd just left. His hair was tousled, the top half of his chest bare, the rest of him covered by crumpled sheets and quilt. He was naked underneath it, she knew, and she again fought the urge to return to the bed.

She forced her attention back to the closet. She needed time and space to think. They'd fallen too easily into the old rhythms of their lovemaking. Who was to say the other old patterns wouldn't follow, including the ones that had destroyed their marriage? It was sweet and easy and wonderful to fall back into bed with him, but the rest would be harder.

With the pink sweater and the skirt in her hand, she took one last backward look. She wanted this, she realized. Maybe she wanted it too much.

She snagged her shoes, then dressed in the bathroom so she wouldn't have to face the temptation of him again. Then, quietly, she slipped out of the house and headed for the shop, where she could remind herself of the woman she'd become. The woman she'd made out of herself, by herself, without Rey.

• • •

Rey wasn't surprised to awaken alone. As wonderful as last night had been, he had expected Joely's over-analyzing nature to prevent a repeat this morning. But that was all right. He could be patient.

As usual in the morning, the house was chillier than he was used to. Shivering, he half ran, still naked, into the living room to dig sweats out of his suitcase. Then he headed to the bathroom to finish his morning routine.

She must have left in a hurry this morning, he reflected as he retrieved some socks. There were no breakfast food smells in the kitchen, and the coffeepot was still cold. He made an omelet for himself, considering his best course of action for the day.

First of all, he wasn't going to rush down to the shop. Now was the time to leave Joely alone, to let her think. No, the best thing he could do today was make himself scarce, possibly for the entire day.

That was fine. It would give him the opportunity to catch up on his work. Plus, he could spend the day planning how to meet Joely tonight when she came home.

That would take some mulling over, to come up with the perfect approach. He pushed it to the back of his mind for the moment. First things first, and the first thing he needed to do was take advantage of the fact he was alone.

He finished his eggs, then cleared off the table and set up his computer. While he was waiting for it to boot up, he picked up his cell phone and dialed his office number.

"Hi, Lisette," he greeted the secretary who answered. "Is Bill in?"

"He's on the phone. Do you want to hold?"

"Sure."

"So how's it going?"

"Fine. Did Bill get the pictures?"

"Yeah. I don't mean with the case, I mean with the other project."

Rey sighed. He didn't really want to discuss this with Lisette. She'd been an important catalyst in Rey's decision to contact Joely while he was working on this case, but he didn't want to think about that right now. Mostly because he knew Joely wouldn't appreciate the story. He hadn't lied about being celibate over the past year, but Lisette had come very close to breaking that trend. Fortunately, she hadn't taken the rejection personally. Unfortunately, she seemed to have adopted him as a sort of pet project.

"So far, so good, I suppose," he said. In spite of having bared his soul to her before, he found himself reluctant now to talk about it. Maybe because he was so focused on Joely now that being so open with another woman seemed wrong. "How long do you think Bill's going to be?"

"I see."

"What do you see?"

"It must be going well if you don't want to talk to me about it."

He laughed, mostly at himself. "I think it's going well. In fact, I think it's going really well."

"Glad to hear it." The warmth in her voice surprised him. He was afraid she might be jealous. Women were funny creatures. "Bill's off the phone. Let me transfer you."

"Rey, the pics are great," Bill said instead of "hello." "I've got things seriously underway, and I'll get back to you as soon as we have all our ducks in line. You did good, Rey."

"Glad to hear it." He drew in a slow breath of cautious relief. They weren't quite done yet, but the case was well underway. If all went as planned, it would be a great coup for him, both professionally and personally. That chapter of his life—and Joely's—would finally be closed.

"Take the rest of the week off," said Bill. "You deserve it. And good luck with that ex-wife thing."

"Jeez." Rey scrubbed his forehead. "Lisette has a big mouth."

"Hey, she likes you. Cut her some slack. Later, Rey."

"Thanks, Bill."

• • •

When Perry arrived, Joely was sitting behind her desk staring at the computer, not entirely sure what she'd been doing before her thoughts had distracted her.

Thoughts of Rey asleep, Rey naked, Rey inside her. About what she should do with Rey next. And no matter how hard she tried to steer her thoughts in other directions, they always ended up with her doing something she shouldn't. Like falling back into Rey's arms without any consideration of where it would take her, or of what it meant for her life here, her shop, her growing success and her new identity.

"What's up, boss?" Perry asked in a typically bright tone. "You look pensive."

Joely looked at her with a grim sigh. "No, just thinking." The joke fell flat, and Perry cocked an eyebrow. Joely shrugged in apology. "Nothing new. Just Rey. Mister 'give me a month to be your husband again.' Mister 'I'm too sexy to live.' Mister 'I know just where to touch you to make all your brains fall out of your head.'" She stopped, not sure if she was about to laugh or cry.

"Rough night, huh?" said Perry with a wry grin.

"I guess that depends on your definition of rough." She put her face in her hands as Perry took the chair on the other side of the desk.

"You want to talk?" Perry offered.

Joely shook her head. "No. But I probably should."

Perry waited patiently for Joely to collect herself. "We were a good couple. I mean, we were a *really* good couple. We had these rhythms, these ways of doing things. It was like we breathed together, like we were one person sometimes."

Perry nodded sagely. "What happened?"

"I was working for a design team for a company that made ceramics. I loved the work, but my boss was a pig. I filed a sexual harassment case. Rey was young and gung-ho, and he insisted on representing me."

Perry made a face. "Ooo. I see what's coming."

"Exactly. Rey was a good lawyer, but he didn't have the experience my boss' lawyer did. He got ripped up one side and down the other in that courtroom. I ended up having to quit my job. After that, it was only a matter of time. He was humiliated, and he threw himself into his work trying to prove himself to his company and, I think, to me. I was devastated, with no job and suddenly no husband, either. It didn't matter to me that he'd lost the case. I knew he'd done the best he could. What mattered to me was having his support while I tried to move on with my life, but he just wasn't there. Finally I got tired of trying to catch his attention, so I threw fake divorce papers at him and left." She shrugged. "Looking back, I don't think I really thought about the consequences."

Perry shook her head. "I don't know what to say."

"There's really nothing *to* say. I just have to decide what I'm going to do about him now."

"Do you want him back?"

"I'm not sure. But I don't think I can send him away. Not now. Not after last night. Maybe not ever."

Perry grinned. "The ol' magic's still there, huh?"

Joely nodded. "There's no thinking things out logically when that kind of thing's going on."

"That's some good sex, then."

"You have no idea." Joely looked back at the computer, moving the mouse a little to deactivate the screensaver. The yearly profit graphs popped back up again, filling the screen. "But I can't forget this. How much of this do I have to give up to keep him? Is there any way I can have both?"

"Do you think he'd want you to go back to New York?"

Joely shook her head. She really wasn't sure. Rey had always seemed to her to thrive on the pace and the atmosphere of New York City, but she supposed it was possible he could change. She had certainly changed, over the last couple of years. Could she change back? Maybe, but it would be terribly painful for her to let go of all the work she'd done here.

Perry settled her chin into the curve of one hand. "It might be worth it, you know."

That, Joely decided, was what scared her the most. "You might be right."

• • •

After he finished the small amount of work he had to do for the day, Rey was at loose ends. With nothing else to do, he paced the living room for a time, until he found himself drinking his third cup of coffee in front of the living room's bay window.

The view was spectacular, still draped with snow, though much had melted in the warmer weather of the past two days. Joely's house appeared to have very little backyard, aside from a small flat area where her barn/studio stood. The property sloped down from the tiny back deck into a pine-filled valley. Beyond it rose more mountains, punctuated with rocky outcroppings. Stretches of green and snow-whitened pine trees alternated with strips of bare, silver trees. The closest patch of these wasn't far from the back of Joely's house. They had white bark, like birches, but he was pretty sure that wasn't what they were. He'd have to ask Joely.

He drained the coffee cup and put it in the sink, then, on a whim, headed out the front door.

The slope of the property wasn't as extreme as it had looked from the house, and he hiked down the edge of the valley to see what he could see. But what impressed him most wasn't so much what he could see, but what he could hear. Or, more accurately, couldn't hear.

No traffic. No sirens. No people sounds at all. He heard birds and squirrels, the wind whispering through the pine needles. The air, saturated with the odor of pine and clean soil, smelled like no one had breathed it in centuries.

He realized suddenly that he'd been standing utterly still for several minutes. It was as if time had stopped. He was so used to seconds and minutes and hours flying by him, so filled with activity he barely knew when one ended and the next began. This was different—time flowing by like slow water, soothing instead of urging him, minutes melting seamlessly from one to the next, but in a way that quieted him instead of speeding him along.

He found a snow-free spot and lowered himself to the ground. It was still damp, and prickly with pine needles, but he didn't mind. Sitting this way, with Joely's house behind him and the wide stretch of rolling mountains in front of him, it was as if he were the only human being on the planet.

He sat for a long time, feeling the wind against his skin, in his hair, listening to the soft, natural sounds, smelling the clean, thin air. The sky above was a rich, sapphire blue, a color he'd never seen in the sky before. Everything tumultuous and anxious inside him stilled and settled. He hadn't felt this peaceful since—actually, he was pretty sure he'd never felt this peaceful before in his life. Unless it was in the womb, and he couldn't remember that.

He'd known from the beginning of this venture that one very large obstacle stood between himself and Joely. Besides his own ego, that is. That was the issue of relocation. He knew that after so long in Colorado, Joely would probably be reluctant to move back to New York. He'd also known that he had no particular desire to leave New York. But today, for the first time, he could picture that happening. It had seemed ridiculous to think he could be happy, or even comfortable, living in the mountains, practically in the middle of nowhere, after a lifetime in the bustling City. But something here touched him deeply.

He had no idea how long he sat there, but finally he realized his foot had fallen asleep. Reluctantly, he stood, stomped it a few times, and continued his walk, to see what other treasures he could find.

• • •

Joely hadn't heard from Rey all day, and drove home suspended between anxiety and anticipation, wondering what he'd been up to, all alone in her house.

Assuming he hadn't made other arrangements, she had a pizza in the back seat of the car. There'd been leftovers from last night, but neither of them had remembered to put them in the refrigerator, and she'd had to toss them in the garbage on her way out this morning. As for dessert—well, there was still the pie, which *had* made it into the fridge. Or, even better, there was Rey.

Though it was a tremendously hard thing for her to do, she'd decided today that she just had to let go. Let things happen as they would without dwelling on where they might lead. More importantly, without trying so hard to be sure they led where she wanted them to go. Rey's return was a gift in and of itself. She should take it, relish it, and be prepared to let it go if necessary. She hoped she wouldn't have to, but if she did, at least if she were prepared, it wouldn't be such a shock to her system.

Rey's rental car still stood in the driveway, but when she went into the house, he was nowhere to be seen.

"Rey?" she called, sliding the pizza onto the table. No answer. "Rey, I'm home!"

Still nothing. Where in the world could he be? Walking to the front bay window, she saw a light on in her workshop. She frowned and headed back outside.

Sure enough, he was in there. He'd helped himself to her supplies and was shaping a piece of clay on her sculpting table. He smiled as she came in.

"Good day at work?"

"Not bad." She gestured toward the table. "What are you doing?"

With a grin, he turned the piece of clay to face her. The shapes were roughly formed, but she could tell what they were supposed to be—two naked figures, one male and one female, in a not-quite-compromising position. "Remind you of anything?" he said.

She smiled and walked toward him. Taking the clay figures from his hand, she turned them, admiring the workmanship, or lack thereof. "Yes, of course it does."

"I really haven't improved any, have I?"

She set the almost-statue back down. "Not a bit."

They'd met in college, when Rey had been in his last year of law school and Joely had been finishing her bachelor's degree in graphic arts. Rey had signed up for a sculpting class specifically to meet girls. Bored by the slow pace of lessons, and completely inept at throwing pots, he'd spent most of his time making naked people. He'd learned nothing whatsoever about sculpting, but he had met Joely, who for whatever reason had found his little statues more endearing than offensive. Maybe because he'd acted out little plays with them, just for her, making her laugh. In return she'd tried to teach him to throw pots, but he'd been hopeless.

Now, six years and one almost-divorce later, he picked the damp statue up and wiggled it. The two figures looked like they were making love, but Rey said in a falsetto voice, "No, move to the right. My bra's hooked on your sweater." Then, in a deeper tone, "Is that better? Ow, you just stuck your boob in my eye."

Joely laughed, covering it with her hand just as if there was a teacher still present to chastise them. He made it easy to remember those days, when they'd just begun to fall in love. It had been crazy then, a sort of elemental force that dragged them both in and wouldn't let them go. Of course, such things faded with time, but here it all was again, the warmth filling her, the trembling in her stomach, the uncertainty about where it would all lead making each moment seem more immediate.

"Show me how to throw a pot," he said.

"No way. Forget it."

He looked hurt. "Why not?"

"Because you'll start singing 'Unchained Melody' and then I'll have to be ill."

He chuckled. It was a good sound—one of the first things she'd noticed about him, she recalled, her memories full now of those days in sculpting class. His chuckle had always sounded genuine, not to mention sexy, with a little bit of gravel to it. "You're right. I probably couldn't resist." They'd reenacted that scene from *Ghost* more than once, usually spoofing it, but still usually also ending up naked. It had finally gotten old, turning into a private joke between them. He'd start humming the song, and she'd roll her eyes and puff out her cheeks, pretending it made her sick.

It might not be so old, now, though. It had been long enough it just might be exciting again.

His smile faded from his mouth, but still crinkled the corners of his eyes as he met her gaze across the room. He was thinking the same thing, she could tell. But suddenly her resolution to let things go as they would wavered. Maybe because this whole situation—the clay, the talking statue—was too firmly rooted in the past. She backed toward the door, still caught in the heat radiating from his eyes.

"I brought home pizza," she said. "Are you hungry?"

He nodded. Looking down, she noticed that he'd pushed the clay figures into each other, wedging them together until one was no longer distinguishable from the other.

"Yeah," he said. "Let's go eat."

· · ·

They were just finishing dinner when Rey said, nonchalantly, "I poked around in the hot tub today."

Joely looked up from her last bite of pizza. "And?"

"It looks to me like the pH levels are okay. How long has it been since you treated the water?"

"I treat it once a week, whether I'm using it or not. Otherwise I have to drain it and start over every time I decide to use it, and that's not fun."

He nodded. "Anyway, I was thinking, what's a trip to Colorado without a dunk in a hot tub?"

She quirked an eyebrow. "I'm guessing you're going for 'incomplete'?"

"Got it in one. What do you say?"

"Did you bring a swimsuit?"

"Do I need one?"

The innocent look in his eyes made her shake her head. "No, I guess you don't."

"Then let's clean this up and get going."

She picked up the nearly empty pizza box and transferred it to the counter. "What about that thirty-minute rule? You know, about swimming after eating."

"This isn't swimming, and that's all a big lie anyway. Don't you keep up with these major health announcements?"

"I guess I missed that one."

She stuffed the last few slices of pizza into a plastic storage bag and put them in the refrigerator. No wasted leftovers tonight. Was that a bad thing or a good thing, that she'd managed to be practical with Rey talking about being naked in the hot tub? She felt like an old married woman, bantering casually about sex without actually doing anything about it.

But wasn't that what she'd wanted to be when she'd married Rey? Eventually, anyway—an old married woman with her old husband next to her, joking about Viagra. It wasn't such a bad place to be. Her parents were like that, and they'd been happily married nearly forty years. Life could be a lot worse.

She went into the living room to find Rey in the process of taking off his underwear. "Are you sure you're okay with this?" he said, balancing on one leg and displaying just about everything he had to offer in the process. "I mean, you seemed a little weird about the clay thing."

She crossed her arms over her chest, enjoying the show as he hopped on one foot, jiggling and bouncing in very interesting places. His erection rose as she looked at it, so she looked at it some more. It continued to harden, forming a lovely arc toward his stomach. His testicles jiggled amusingly for a few seconds, then stilled as they tightened. As well as she'd known him, she'd never watched this process in stark light, and it intrigued her. She smiled. Rey looked distinctly uncomfortable.

"That's because it's impossible to get clay out of your clothes," she said.

That wasn't the only reason, though. This was the new Rey, not the old, college-aged Rey he'd tried to recreate before. If she was going to move ahead, it had to be with the new version. In this, as in all other things in life, there was no going back.

He rolled his underwear into a ball and tossed it into the pile with his other clothes. "Aren't you going to join me?"

"Yeah. Just a minute."

She unbuttoned her blouse as he opened the door, thoroughly enjoying the sight of his tight, naked ass as he walked away from her, toward the door to the deck. *That* hadn't changed much. She was glad it hadn't. He'd always had a fine ass.

She took off her shirt and tossed it on top of Rey's clothes, then went to grab some towels before she forgot.

Joely had never spent a great deal of time in the hot tub, and when she had, it had usually been for therapeutic reasons—loosening back muscles clenched from too many hours on her feet at the shop, or just for stress relief. She'd never had anyone else in it until now. So, even though she rarely wore a suit in the tub, and even though it was Rey who sat there waiting for her to get in, she felt a little self-conscious as she laid the towels down on the deck, then climbed up the two wooden stairs to step into the water. Rey watched her with an appreciative smile.

"Is this too hot?" he asked. "I turned the thermostat up a little."

"No, it's fine." It was warmer than she usually kept it, but not uncomfortable. She settled into one of the tub's molded plastic seats and reached over to turn on the jets. Pulsing streams of water began to pound against her back, just hard enough to feel good after a long day of work.

"Mmm," said Rey. "That's nice."

She looked toward him to see him with his eyes half closed, wriggling against the sensation of the water jets. The sight aroused her instantly. She crossed her legs against the hot, wet need pooling between them. It didn't help—the friction just increased the sensation, and the hot water of the tub aroused her that much more. She wanted him inside her so badly, wanted him deep, wanted him to take her hard up against the side of the tub—

He opened his eyes and looked back at her, a wicked grin curling the sensuous curves of his mouth. "No wonder you haven't needed a man around. You've had this hot tub. I'm jealous." He moved sinuously against the jet she knew was right behind him, and she couldn't help but wonder exactly where he was directing the sharp, pulsing current.

She gathered herself. "Yes, a girl can have many of her emotional and sexual needs filled by a large plastic bucket of hot water equipped with pulsating jets," she said wryly.

His grin deepened, and wickedness flashed in his eyes. "You're a very bad girl. I like that." Lifting a hand out of the water, he beckoned to her. "C'mere."

She tilted him a skeptical look, but half-floated her way across the tub to sit next to him. His arm closed around her waist and he drew her tight against him, his mouth seeking hers.

There was no point even thinking about resisting him. Her hands clutched at his shoulders as his lips pressed against hers, softly at first, exploring. He kissed her as if it were the first time he'd ever done so, as if there were a million new, small sensations to find there in the meeting of his lips with hers. One hand moved up from her waist to cup her breast, rolling her taut nipple against the middle of his palm. Desire shot through her and she moaned low in her throat, pushing herself closer to him. She was already so hot, so slick. She felt like if she breathed the right way, she would fall into orgasm.

She hooked a knee over his bare hip, half-straddling him. Her sex opened against his thigh and she pulsed her hips, dragging her sex against the rough hair of his leg. The sensation sent her higher, skirting the edges of pure ecstasy. She moaned into his mouth.

Suddenly, Rey's gentleness departed and he dove into the kiss like a starving man. Joely met the sudden surge of passion, opening her mouth to his questing tongue, pressing her body harder against his. His thumbs flicked her nipples, stinging the sensitive flesh, then he pulled his mouth away from hers to close it over her breast. His tongue took over where his thumb had left off, his greedy mouth suckling, teeth scraping over her nipples. He bit her softly and she cried out at the sharp lance of pain, but when he started to draw back, she held his head still.

"Don't stop."

He didn't. He bit her nipple again and she flinched, digging her fingers into his hair. Drawing her breast deep into his mouth, he sucked her hard, until she shuddered with the intense sensation, her voice keening in her throat.

"God, Rey…"

He pulled his head back and looked up into her eyes. She looked back, into the warm, deep gray, and the love there made tears spring to her eyes.

His hands slipped under her, lifting her hips away from the bottom of the tub. The water pushed her up, and she let herself go, until she was floating next to him. He shifted with her, one hand sliding down her stomach until he cupped her sex, his fingers questing, stroking her.

One finger dipped inside her, then two, and she gasped. With her body floating, it was as if she had become nothing but the flame he had ignited there between her legs. He pressed his fingers in and out of her, slowly, then harder, firmer. He curled the tips up, and when he touched her there, pressed hard, a sharp, sensation stabbed through her, pain but not pain, so intense she could barely contain it. She jumped, gasped, grabbed his shoulder with one hand to steady herself. She heard him laugh.

He worked the spot for a time, watching her face, smiling, then his thumb found her swollen, hungry center and circled it, softly, then more firmly until, caught up in the sensation, she rose in a sudden rush and toppled over the edge. He held her while she did it, and when she came back to herself, he was smiling at her.

Still overcome by the intensity of her climax, Joely managed to get her legs under her again and reached for Rey. She closed her fingers around his shaft, finding it steely hard and ready for her. She stroked him once, then he stopped her with a touch.

"Back inside," he said. "I want to be inside you, and I forgot to bring the condoms."

"Do they even work underwater?" she asked as he lifted her in his arms, hauling her out of the hot tub. She shuddered as the chilly night air hit the water on her skin. The change in temperature was a definite shock, a deep, pervasive, sensual sensation in and of itself, as every inch of her responded, every nerve ending jolted to alertness.

Either he didn't hear her query about the condoms, or he wasn't interested in the answer, because he didn't say anything. He deposited her on the deck, then grabbed a towel and wrapped it around her. She'd barely managed to adjust it over her breasts when he picked her up again, carrying her back into the house.

He set her down in the kitchen, where she toweled herself off quickly, trying not to drip too much onto the wooden floor.

She didn't think she'd ever seen him so single-minded. He took no more than a few seconds to swipe himself with the towel before he half ran into the living room to grab a condom from the couch. He'd remembered them, apparently—he just hadn't remembered to bring them outside.

He tossed the square packet to her and she tore it open. When she looked up, he was standing in front of her. He grabbed her shoulders and kissed her hard, his mouth questing deep into hers, tongue probing. His mouth was hot after the shock of the cold outside air. Her towel started to slip down and he readjusted it, holding it against her shoulders. After a time, he drew back and pressed his forehead against hers.

She drew a steadying breath. "Right here?" she asked.

"Right here," he said, his voice rasping with need.

She smiled and looked down. He was fully, achingly erect. Seeing it made need jolt from her groin to her chest, need to take him in, to feel him take her, deep and hard. Reaching down, she unrolled the condom over him. It seemed a shame, almost, to cover him up. Pretty, she thought, the shapes and contours, right down to the blue veins tracing the shaft.

He left her little time, though, to admire it. Condom in place, he grasped her by the waist and deposited her on the kitchen counter. She cocked her legs over his hips and he plunged inside.

For a moment, he held still, sheathed deeply inside her. She could feel every inch of him, the tip pressing against her womb, sending a slow wave of heat up through her chest.

She let him stay there for a long breath, then nudged his hips with her calves, pushing him closer, even farther inside, though that had not seemed possible. A moan wrenched its way out of his throat and he pulled out, then pressed back in, starting an irresistible rhythm.

She'd finished once, in the hot tub, but the heat rose inside her again, rising and pulsing until she found herself in the tide of another climax. His thrusts quickened, harder and deeper, as her body tightened on him, and when she toppled for the second time, he joined her. She pushed herself closer to him, pulled him in as deep as she could, feeling the steady, heavy pulse of his ejaculation.

She felt suspended outside her own body as the waves passed over her, as she clenched and eased on him. Finally, he lowered his head and kissed her hair.

"I love you," he said.

She opened her mouth to answer him but nothing came out. A thick clog of tears had filled her throat. Closing her mouth, she swallowed hard, feeling a hot tear wind its way down her cheek. He only smiled, and kissed the tear away.

Chapter Nine

She woke early again, comfortably cocooned in the warm blankets next to Rey. While he snored softly next to her, she snuggled against him, pressing her bare breasts against his back. He shifted a little. She tucked her chin into the curve of his shoulder and lightly kissed his ear.

"Good morning," she whispered, softly enough it wouldn't wake him if he were deeply asleep.

He made an odd, very unromantic snorting noise. "Morinn," he mumbled, then rolled over to face her, wrapped his arms around her and apparently fell headlong back to sleep again.

She smiled. He should have been awake and raring to go, with the two-hour time difference between here and New York. His jet lag seemed to be working in the wrong direction. She settled down into his embrace and closed her eyes.

A moment later, he sat up. "It's time for you to go to work, isn't it?"

She looked into his bleary eyes and realized she never wanted to get out of this bed again. "It's okay. It's Sunday. It's my only day off."

He nodded and lay back down, closing his eyes again.

She grinned. "You sure you want to sleep, hon?" she said.

Opening one eye, he regarded her with interest, more awake than he'd been a few seconds ago. "You had something else in mind?"

She slipped her hand down his stomach. "Maybe."

He growled and grabbed her. She laughed as he rolled on top of her, pushing her down into the bed.

It was indescribably delicious to have a man in her bed again, Joely thought as his talented hands began their work, drawing lines of fire over her body, arousing her breasts, gently invading and rousing her. No, not just any man. *This* man. This man who could make her feel so wanton and so safe at the same time. Who knew exactly where and how to touch her to start that hot ecstasy spiraling inside her, and how to nurture it until it filled her and overflowed. Who knew without asking that she wanted him to look into her eyes as he came hard inside her, and to keep looking as he, too, toppled over the peak.

And there was more than fire in his eyes when he did it. She thought she'd seen it last night, but it had been hard to tell in the semi-darkness. Love. He could speak it all he wanted, but seeing it dark and heavy in his gray eyes made her want to weep.

But she didn't, not this time. She drowned herself in it, watching him climax, until he finally closed his eyes to ride her on the final, overwhelming waves. Then, when he sighed and looked at her again, she kissed him gently on lips still trembling a little.

"I love you, too," she whispered.

He smiled, and closed his arms around her, and cradled her against his heartbeat.

• • •

Later, she poured Rey a cup of coffee while his eggs were cooking. He sipped at it, eyeing her through a misplaced lock of dark hair. Wearing sweats and no socks, unshaven and tousled from early-morning lovemaking, he looked tremendously sexy.

"I have a question for you, Rey," she said, sliding the finished eggs into a plate. She set the plate down in front of him and picked up her own plate of toast.

"Shoot," he said.

"If all this works out, where are we going to live?"

He considered a moment, but he didn't look particularly perturbed by the question. "I guess we'd have to work that out."

"Yes, we would. Do you have any thoughts on the subject?"

"I've never lived outside New York," he said. Her heart sank, but he wasn't finished. "However, I think I might like it here. I could find work in Denver, or I could even help you out with your business."

She chewed her lip, almost afraid to believe he was really saying this. "You'd be willing to move?"

"Yeah, I think so." He paused. "Would you?"

This caught her off-guard. She hadn't expected him to turn the question back on her. "Honestly, Rey, I don't know. I've worked really hard to do what I've done here. I don't know if I could give it up."

He nodded. "Well, one of us has to make the sacrifice, and since I'm the one who screwed things up in the first place, it might as well be me."

"Rey—"

He held up a hand. "It's all hypothetical right now, anyway, isn't it? We have a month to think it all through."

She nodded. "You're right."

Still, his willingness to consider leaving New York gave her a new sense of optimism. If he could make that big a change for her, it seemed that much more likely that he'd make an extra effort to be sure things went well from there. She chewed her toast, watching him eat his eggs, and considered another possible piece to the plan.

"Tomorrow, when we go in," she finally said, "you could look over my books and tell me what you think. We could come up with some ideas about how we could work together."

He nodded. "That sounds like a good idea." He reached across the table and squeezed her hand. "So what do you want to do today?"

"I want to show you Colorado. I want to show you why I stayed."

• • •

It was too cold to hike, so she took him for a drive. West down highway 285, through Shawnee to Grant, where she turned to head up Guanella Pass.

She'd only been this way once, last spring. It was too late in the year to see the stands of aspens in glittering gold, but the scenery was still incredible. The road twisted and turned, switching back on itself time after time as it wound its way up and over the ridge of mountains. With each hairpin curve, a new vista was revealed—here a waterfall, here a grand sweep of evergreen forest, here the massive slope of a snow-covered mountain.

The road became iffier as they neared the top. Joely trusted her own driving and the Jeep's four-wheel drive. Rey clutched the edges of the seat as the road became little more than raw rock, throwing the Jeep back and forth alarmingly. At least, apparently, for Rey, who kept his eyes fixed on the often steep drop-offs, sometimes out his window, sometimes out Joely's.

At the top of the pass, she pulled the Jeep over. There was a path here where you could hike up Mount Bierstadt, one of several fourteeners—fourteen-thousand foot peaks—in the area.

"What do you think?" Joely asked.

"It's beautiful," he said. He sounded sincere, and when she looked at him she saw appropriate awe on his face. "It really is. I can see why you love it. It must feed your artistic muse."

"Yes, it does." She took a long breath, letting the spell of the place settle over her.

They sat in silence for a time, then Joely turned, surprised, as Rey's hand settled over hers. "Not much traffic up here, is there?"

"Not this time of year. It gets busier over the su—"

She broke off as his mouth closed on hers. He kissed her, soft and warm and deep, then drew back with a wicked smile.

"How far off-road can you get this thing?"

"As far as I like, I suppose. I don't want to get stuck in the snow, though."

"Hey, it's a Jeep. Show a little adventurous spirit."

She knew full well where his mind was. The idea appealed to her. A lot. She reached toward the gearshift but caught his thigh instead. "I can get us far enough."

With the Jeep in low gear, she trundled over the uneven, snowy ground until they were shielded by a stand of evergreens.

"Back seat?" he said, mischief in his eyes.

"Damn straight," she answered, adjusting the driver's seat as she spoke, moving it forward as far as it would go.

Braving the cold, they got out and climbed into the back seat. Before Joely had quite closed the door, Rey had caught hold of her, dragging her across the back seat, half into his lap. He kissed her, devouring her mouth while his hands slid down her back, cupped her ass. His tongue pressed in, tangling with hers.

Joely laughed. "What?" Rey said, almost as if in protest.

She shook her head, unable really to explain. It just struck her funny, that they were about to make love in the backseat of a car, like teenagers afraid of getting caught by their parents.

He grinned at her, eyes twinkling, and she sensed that he understood. She smiled back. That was the way they had always been—in synch, practically reading each other's minds. It felt good to have that back.

She grappled with the snap on his jeans, with the zipper, finding it quite difficult to get them unfastened while he was sitting. But she managed to get them open, and to work the jeans down his hips and partway down his thighs. He was already firmly erect, and as she worked the jeans down, he worried a rather bent condom package out of his pocket and laid it on the seat next to him.

She smiled up at him, not sure why that particular gesture touched her so much. Maybe because it proved he'd planned ahead, or maybe because it proved he was thinking about protecting her. Either way, it made her warm. Made her love him.

She maneuvered into an uncomfortable sitting position on the floor between the driver's seat and the back seat. She'd positioned the driver's seat to its farthest forward position, so there was some room, but it wasn't quite enough. Still, she could make do. She adjusted until she was relatively comfortable, sitting between Rey's open knees. He looked down at her, heavy-lidded, lips slightly parted, and put his hand on her head, combing his fingers into her hair. He knew what was coming. Not forcing it, but obviously anticipating it.

She smiled. Tenting her fingertips against his knees, she traced them up his thighs, then back down. His eyes closed and he let his head settle back against the headrest with a soft sigh of contentment.

She slipped her fingers again along his thighs, up to his belly, dropped a fingertip into his navel, lifted it back out again, carefully circumnavigating even the dark curls of his pubic hair. Then, with no preamble, she bent and took him into her mouth. He jumped, gasped, and she chuckled, licking him.

He filled her mouth as well as he did her body, and the taste of his skin brought back memories of other back seats, other blowjobs, quickly going down on him behind bushes at dusk on the college quad. She took him in, deep, all the way to the back of her throat, smiling at the way he fit perfectly against the back of her palate. She had missed that. They fit together like puzzle pieces.

His hands fisted gently in her hair and he began to pulse his hips. It felt good. He tasted good. Faster, deeper, and she brought up a hand to curl her fingers around him as he thrust, working his skin, feeling the hardness beneath it. Then, abruptly, he stopped, and drew her head up.

"Inside," he said. "I want to come inside you."

She nodded, then looked around at the narrow confines of the Jeep. How had they done this, years ago? How did teenagers manage? Was it just because they were skinnier?

"Turn around," he said.

She did, with some difficulty, ending up positioned in the space between front and back seats, facing toward the front window. She stood, more or less, bent over the front seat with the back of her head against the roof.

He laughed. "You don't look very comfortable."

"I'm not." She couldn't help smiling; it was all really fairly ludicrous.

"I'll fix that," he assured her.

He reached around her and unfastened her jeans, sliding them slowly down her hips. He leaned in as he did so, tracing his tongue down her back until it touched the top of the cleft between her buttocks. She shivered under the soft, wet contact. He withdrew, then blew gently on the trail he had left behind. She laughed.

"Damn, that's cold."

He laughed, too, then cupped his hands around her hips and settled her back toward him.

She moved with him, trusting him. He maneuvered her backward, one hand steadying her while the other reached between her legs, his fingers sliding inside her. She closed her eyes, the better to feel the penetration, as his fingers went in deep, as far as they could go. Then they slid out, and his erection took their place, sliding inside.

Rey brought her gently back, at the same time rising behind her. There was a handle on the Jeep's ceiling, just above the door, for extra stability during rough off-road travel. Rey took hold of it as he lifted himself from the back seat, using it as leverage as he pushed deep into Joely from behind.

Joely braced herself against the front seat. She was cold but she didn't care; Rey was inside her and she could feel his hot belly against her back.

"You good?" he asked.

"Good," she managed. Good didn't cover it. Fantastic, wonderful, transcendent…There were no words. He was just—inside. Part of her. Irrevocably.

"Good," he repeated, and braced himself, and began to thrust.

It was awkward, but the awkwardness enhanced it. She looked out the open window at the snow, the trees, and the thought that someone could wander in and walk right up to the car and watch them made her hot and buttery. God, he felt good inside her, stabbing deep, taking her. He could possess her so completely, so easily. No wonder she'd never wanted another man the way she'd always wanted Rey. The way she wanted him now.

Deeper, harder, the tempo increasing. Joely reached up to close her hand over his, on the handle above the door, her fingers digging tight into his hand. He was pounding into her, hard, and finally she reached down and touched herself.

"I want to feel you come," Rey said, his voice low and insistent, and she nodded. She was almost there, it wouldn't take much—and sure enough, she suddenly felt herself open up, as if something were rising and bursting under her finger, filling her whole body with slow, easy waves of molten heat.

"God," she whispered. Rey made a small, breathy sound, and shoved into her hard, and held still, except for the sharp, small movements of his pelvis, and the pulsation Joely could feel inside her as he emptied.

Finally, finished, his breath still fast and ragged, he gathered her against him. "Joely, that was—"

But he stopped then, abruptly.

"What?" she said.

"Shh." He reached around her, touching her lips with his fingertips. "I saw something."

She peered out the side window. "A person?" she whispered.

"I don't know." He pulled her jeans into place as he drew back from her, covering her. He didn't seem as concerned about his own state of dishabille. The gesture touched her.

They held still for what seemed a very long time before Rey suddenly let out a long breath. "Look." He pointed.

She looked. Emerging from among the trees was a herd of elk. She saw five now, but there were more, and they moved slowly out of the trees, down the mountain toward the open area next to the road where they could graze. One after another they came, most of them cows, but one or two bearing short, spiky antlers.

"Wow," Rey breathed. "They're gorgeous. I had no idea they were so big."

She laid her hands over his and leaned back into him, savoring the moment.

They fell silent again as the rest of the herd passed. Three of them stopped, peering at the car with wide, calm eyes. Finally, they went on with the others, apparently deciding the unmoving Jeep wasn't a threat.

"That's it," said Joely. "That's why I stayed here."

He nodded slowly. "I think I would have, too."

• • •

They spent the evening in the hot tub again, but this time they didn't make love. He sat next to her, watching her feet float, his fingers tangled with hers. Above them the night sky was black and clear, scattered with stars that looked close enough to touch.

"There are so many," he said, his voice barely more than a breath.

"It's the altitude. The air's thinner. Plus, there aren't any streetlights."

Rey had never seen the Milky Way look so milky. For a moment, the vast star field overwhelmed him. Then Joely's fingers moved in his and he was grounded again.

Later, lying in bed next to her, he felt much the same way. Overwhelmed, just for a moment, by the depth of emotion that overtook him at the sight of her sleeping face. Then, as she moved closer to him, one arm falling across his waist, a sudden sense that everything was as it should be.

He folded her in his arms, cradling her warmth against him. This was all he really needed. The rest—where to live, where to work—was nothing compared to this.

He couldn't ask for anything more.

Except maybe—just maybe—a little more heat in the house

• • •

The next morning after breakfast, they went to the shop and spent several hours looking over Joely's computer records. Rey focused on the financial spreadsheets, printing out everything from Joely's opening day to the present. He became so wrapped up in what he was doing that finally she gave up any attempt at recapturing his attention. Instead she went out front to help Perry with the customers.

"What's he doing back there?" Perry asked. The shop was quiet at the moment, and she was replenishing the cash register's supply of pennies.

"Looking over my spreadsheets." She unlocked the back of the jewelry case and straightened some turquoise necklaces that weren't quite the way she wanted them. "He wants to see how he can help with the business if he stays here."

Perry's eyebrows rose. "Really? He's thinking about staying?"

"It sounds like it's a possibility."

"So, you guys are really getting back together?" She shook the last few stubborn pennies out of the paper roll and closed the cash drawer. "I'm happy for you, Joely."

Joely shrugged. "I'm not completely sure it's going to happen yet, but it looks promising." She looked wistfully toward the office door. "Especially if he's willing to stay here. He'd be giving up a lot."

"Well, you'd be giving up a lot if you went with him to New York, too."

"I know. And I'm not sure I could do that for him. But he says he can do this for me. That's big."

"Yes, it is. But that's good, right?"

But Joely frowned, a sudden, unpleasant thought intruding.

"What?" asked Perry.

"It's too big, maybe. Too much, too fast." She crossed her arms tightly across her chest, trying to squeeze the optimism back into herself. Too late—it had drained away as if someone had pulled the cork out of the bottom of her psyche.

Perry shook her head, rolling her eyes. "Why are you doing this? Why can't you just be happy, without worrying about everything so much?"

Joely gave her friend a tired smile. "It's just me. Once bitten, twice shy. It's hard for me to trust him again."

"Well, just do it. I think he's ready to take the plunge."

But something still nagged at Joely, some question she couldn't quite put words to, but which she was certain hadn't been sufficiently answered. She sighed, trying to let all her doubts and uncertainties dissipate with the long breath.

"Maybe you're right. He seems genuine."

"He loves you, Joely."

"That was never the question. Unfortunately, that's not quite enough."

Perry looked deflated. "It should be."

• • •

Rey surfaced again at lunchtime, offering to fetch takeout for all three of them. When he got back, Joely and Perry joined him in the office, leaving the door propped open so they could hear any customers who might drop in. He'd brought back Chinese food complete with chopsticks, so the women sat maneuvering the sticks around slippery lo mein noodles while Rey used his utensils mostly for punctuation while he talked.

"You've done almost no advertising, did you know that?" he said to Joely.

"Of course I know that."

"And in spite of that, your business has increased by almost three hundred percent since you opened last September."

Joely shrugged. "It's mostly word-of-mouth. That's what works best up here."

"Do you realize what you could do if you pumped a little money into your advertising budget? With that kind of growth from word-of-mouth, you could skyrocket if you took out a few ads."

"I don't know that it would make that much difference. I talked to several of the local merchants up here, and they said advertising revenue wasn't always the best way to spend your money."

He started to speak, then stopped. She could tell he was regrouping his thoughts. He took the few moments to snag some lo mein. Perry, Joely noticed, was watching with interest and amusement.

"Then we should look into that," Rey finally went on. "Ask around, look at some numbers. There's got to be some way to make an advertising budget work for you."

"Maybe some promotional events, rather than traditional advertising," Perry put in.

Rey pointed his chopsticks at her. "Good idea. We'll keep you."

"I should hope so!" Perry exclaimed, indignant. Rey winked at her.

"Don't tease Perry," said Joely. "Besides, you'd have to walk over my dead body to fire her."

"Which would be quite unpleasant." He attended to his food again, brow creased in a thoughtful frown. "What about this commission thing? Maybe you could pay some of your artisans a flat fee to produce a certain amount of merchandise rather than paying them a percentage per sale."

"Might work, might not. It would take some time to figure out what numbers would work. And I might lose some artisans over it."

"Not if we made it optional." He shook his head. "Just throwing out ideas. I think you've got a great thing going here, Joely."

She smiled. His enthusiasm was not only infectious, but encouraging. If he was this excited about her business, then maybe he really could commit to staying in Colorado. She'd been afraid leaving New York might mean also leaving a job he felt passionately about, but there was passion here now, as well.

"Here's another idea," he went on. "We could set up a website and you could sell your pieces online. With a couple of people to handle orders—more later, of course—we could get national distribution. International, even."

"You're thinking awfully big there, Rey." She pictured herself making pots twenty-four seven. She liked her work, but too much of anything could get old.

"We have to think big," he countered. "It wouldn't all fall on you, of course. We could sell other people's work, as well, just like you're doing now, and everybody's stuff would be in limited runs to drive up the value. You know, limited edition numbered pieces, that kind of thing. That way we keep the quality up."

Perry nodded. "Great ideas, Rey. When do we talk about Christmas bonuses and stock options, that kind of thing?"

"We have to have stock before we can have stock options," said Rey, then saw Perry's grin. "You're mocking me." His offense was mostly feigned.

"Never," Perry answered. "I just enjoy watching you come up with all these ideas that could eventually make me a lot of money." In the showroom, the bell on the door tinkled. "I'll get that."

Rey watched her go. "I like her. We can definitely keep her.'

"Like I said, Perry's not going anywhere."

Rey looked at her, the expression, his eyes changing from mirth to affection. "With any kind of luck, neither am I."

Joely smiled, a soft thrill of arousal moving through her body, combined with affection that made the emotion just short of lethal. But something still nagged. What was the question? The question she hadn't asked, but should have? It was there, lurking around the edges of everything they did and said, but she couldn't quite figure out what it was.

She would though, eventually. When she did, she hoped it didn't ruin everything.

• • •

Rey had made a stack of notes during the afternoon, to remind himself of ideas he'd had while going over Joely's files. He could set up some spreadsheets on his own computer, to make projections and see what kinds of things he might recommend. He'd minored in accounting in college, and his work as a corporate lawyer had exposed him to a good number of business types. He thought his ideas would be as valuable as anyone else's.

Not that Joely wouldn't have come up with many of them on her own, given time. But it couldn't hurt to have another brain on the job, and another body to carry out the work.

He had just gotten seriously underway when Joely poked her head into the office. "Could you keep an eye on things for a bit?"

"What's up?"

Joely looked a little sheepish. "I mean, if you don't mind. Tara just got a new shipment of these gorgeous crystal jewelry pieces and she asked if Perry and I would like to bip next door to look at them."

He smiled. "Sure. Go ahead. I'll hold down the fort."

Things were quiet, but he did sell a few items over the next quarter of an hour. One was a large sale—one of Joely's wolf-themed vases. He almost hated to let it go, it was so representative of her work. He'd always liked her work.

Straightening the cash in the drawer, he gave the store a quick scan. A man stood across the room, perusing Joely's other wolf pieces. Rey hadn't seen him come in—he must have been busy ringing up another customer. He closed the cash drawer and settled onto the stool behind the counter.

Five minutes later, the man was still there. Which wasn't a big deal if he was just browsing, but why would a serious browser stand staring at the same two pots for five solid minutes? Warning bells went off in Rey's head. Probably just paranoia inspired by the case Bill had sent him out here to settle, but, in Rey's opinion, you couldn't be too careful. He slid off the stool and came out from behind the counter.

"May I help you?" he asked the man.

The customer jumped, then grinned sheepishly. He looked at Rey over his shoulder. "I'm sorry. You startled me."

Rey took a step closer. The customer had something in his hands, Rey was certain. Otherwise, he would have turned around all the way, instead of holding this awkward pose with his head turned toward Rey and his hands both kept stiffly between his body and the merchandise shelves.

"What are you doing?" Rey asked, though he was fairly sure he knew.

"Just admiring this beautiful work." The man shifted, sliding a hand into his coat pocket.

"What was that?"

"What was what?"

"What did you just put in your pocket?"

The man had the nerve to look affronted. "I don't think that's any of your business."

"And I think it is." He stepped a little closer, looming over the smaller man. "You want to show me?"

"I most certainly do not."

The man's indignation only made Rey angry. "Then how about let's play a little game. I think you just dropped a camera in your pocket. I think you were taking pictures of the merchandise."

"Why in the world would I do that?"

"You work for Cherokee Ceramics?"

Bingo. The man flushed. Obviously, his boss had picked entirely the wrong person to go on this particular mission. "I am deeply offended by your behavior, sir. Would you like to speak to my lawyer?"

"Yes, actually, I would. Why don't you give me his number?'

With a huff, the man stormed out of the store. As luck would have it, he stormed right past Joely and Perry, coming back in.

"What was that all about?" Joely asked. She tilted an eyebrow at Rey, as if she thought he might have deliberately lost her a customer.

"Little creep tried to steal something," he muttered.

Which was precisely the truth. He only regretted he hadn't been able to get hold of the camera, and dispose of the pictures he was certain the "customer" had taken.

•••

It surprised him, as they drove home, how he'd started to think of this place as home. He hadn't even been here a week, and it felt as natural as breathing to watch the mountains roll by, feel his ears pop a little as they spiraled up the road to Joely's house. To walk into Joely's house and think of it as his own.

He laid his computer down on the coffee table while Joely headed for the bedroom to change her clothes. Looking around, he calculated the size of the house. It was cozy, but they might want something larger in a year or two. And it would be nice to have a yard for the kids—

He cut that thought off. He was getting too far ahead of himself. First, he had to be sure Joely was ready to take the plunge back into marriage.

He had some thoughts about that, too. They'd never officially been divorced, but he thought it would be nice to have a little ceremony of some kind when they got back together. Nothing formal, just something to celebrate the fact that he'd finally come to his senses.

He kicked off his shoes and stretched out on the couch. Yes, this was good. Very good. He could get used to this in a big hurry.

Joely came back into the living room, wearing cotton lounge pants and a T-shirt with no bra. He smiled at this sign she was getting comfortable with him again. "C'mere," he said, waving to her.

"Don't you want dinner?"

"Eventually. I'm not really that hungry, to tell the truth." She came to him and he rolled onto his side to make room for her on the couch. He could have sat up, he supposed, but it was cozier this way, with him lying down and Joely sitting with her round bottom tucked against his stomach. "You're an amazing woman, did you know that?"

"Yes, I did. But what makes you say that?"

"I don't think I could have done such a thorough or successful job of remaking myself as you have. You've really accomplished something here. I'm very impressed."

"Thank you." She smiled, brushing hair back out of his eyes, then abruptly sobered. "Tell me, Rey. Honestly, now. If you left New York and came to live here, what would you lose?"

He shrugged. "Besides my job? Nothing."

"But your job's always been important to you."

"Too important. I need to change that." But his answer had come too quickly and too firmly, and he knew it.

The truth was, he hadn't taken nearly enough time to evaluate what he wanted to do. He'd been focused on what Joely wanted him to do, and what would be the most expedient way to mend their relationship.

"What are you doing now?" Joely pressed on. "What's changed with you since the last time I saw you?"

"Well..." He wasn't sure this was a direction he wanted this conversation to go. "I've handled several very successful cases. One was a sexual harassment case at a major company." She looked away at this. He couldn't blame her. "Bill's talked about making me a partner."

"Do you still live in our old apartment?"

"No. I found a nice place in Manhattan."

"Expensive. So you're making a lot more money than you were when I left." She paused significantly. "A lot more than you could ever hope to make if you moved out here."

She'd backed him right into that one. "Yeah, but the cost of living's a lot lower out here. We'd get by just fine."

"But would you be happy? Would you really and truly be happy helping me expand my business? Is that really what you want to do with your life?"

"This is an essay question," he grumbled. "I'm way better at multiple choice."

"Okay, choice A—go back to New York without me. Choice B—I move to New York with you. Choice C—move to Colorado and help me with my business. Choice D—move to Colorado and work downtown for a corporate law firm. What's your first choice?"

The answer surprised even him. "This is silly, Joely."

"Tell me, Rey." The expression on her face was fiercely demanding.

He had to say it. She wasn't going to let him get away with anything else. "Honestly, it would have to be B—you move to New York with me."

"That's what I thought."

"But C and D are completely acceptable."

"Are you absolutely sure?"

He nodded firmly. "Yes."

Her eyes had gone sad. He wondered why, until she said, "Then you're a better person than I am. Truly, Rey. Because I don't think I could ever do choice B."

She pushed away from him, to her feet, and walked slowly into the bedroom. The door closed softly behind her. Rey put his face in his hands and sighed. Why did she have to make this so impossible?

After a few minutes, he got up and followed her into the bedroom. She was stretched out flat on her back on the bed, staring blankly at the ceiling.

"It's okay, Joely," he said gently. "You don't have to want choice B."

She turned her head a little to look at him. Her eyes were rimmed with red. "It's not that I don't want choice B. It's that there's no way in a million years that I could go back to New York with you and be happy. Not now. Not after what I've done here. And that's wrong of me, because if you're willing to give up what you've built in New York, I should be willing to give up what I've built here, for the sake of our marriage."

"That doesn't make you a bad person."

"Yes, it does."

He sank onto the bed next to her and took her hand, closing both of his over it. She had big hands for a woman, but she was tall and they didn't look out of proportion on her. Besides, they were long, slim hands, with long fingers that could curl around a lump of clay and shape it to perfection.

"What I built in New York I can build again here. But what you have here—I don't think you could do the same thing in New York. I mean, you could have a little boutique, maybe, and be successful at it, but it wouldn't be the same."

"Would being a corporate lawyer in Denver be the same as being a corporate lawyer in New York?"

"No, but being a lawyer is different from being an artist. Something here speaks to your soul. I can see it in your work. The stuff you did before you came out here was good, but this new work is exceptional. You belong here. I couldn't ask you to leave, knowing that. Besides, like I said before, I'm the one who screwed up. I'm the one who needs to make amends. Therefore, I'm the one who needs to make whatever sacrifices are necessary."

She nodded, but she didn't look convinced. "It just seems too good to be true. Too fast, too perfect."

Gently, he slid a hand over her hair. The short blonde strands were soft against his palm. "The month's not up yet. We won't decide on anything until it is."

"Okay. That's a deal."

He squeezed her hand. "How about some of that leftover pizza?"

• • •

They ate leftover pizza, then Rey had Joely stretch out on the couch while he massaged her feet. He knew they must be tired after the day at the shop, but he hadn't anticipated the rest of her being tired, as well. He'd barely finished one foot when he realized she'd fallen asleep.

Well, so much for another night of passionate sex. He'd have to take a rain check. Gently, he scooped her up from the couch and carried her into the bedroom. As he lowered her onto the bed, she opened her eyes and looked at him, smiled, and closed her eyes again. He doubted she'd been awake at all.

The covers were still mussed from last night—and this morning—which was fortunate because otherwise he would never have been able to get her under them. He tucked them around her, then undressed and slid in after her. Still without waking up, she rolled toward him, curling her warmth against him as he settled into the mattress.

Just like old times. He'd decided, over the last, long months of being alone, that he'd give up almost anything to have this back. Even New York. Even a possible partnership at his law firm.

Joely had pillowed her head against his shoulder and he traced his finger down her cheek, savoring the softness of her skin. He could lie like this all night, he thought, just watching her sleep.

Everything was going perfectly, he reflected as he drifted into sleep, himself. Exactly according to plan.

Chapter Ten

He woke before she did, for a change. Faced with this novel situation, his first instinct was to nudge her, or caress her, or in some other way to gently awaken her so they could make love.

His hand was inches away from her breast when he hesitated. Sex was a pretty obvious route to take at this point. Maybe he should try something different. As he looked at her quietly sleeping face, the answer came to him. He could make breakfast.

As much as Joely liked to eat breakfast out, he knew she liked it even better when someone made it for her. So, resisting the temptation of her sleeping self, he rolled out of bed and got dressed. In the kitchen, he poked through her cabinets, found a bag of pancake mix, and got started.

The kitchen was full of the smells of coffee, bacon, and cooking pancakes when Joely meandered in, bleary-eyed and smiling.

"Wow," she said. "You're making breakfast?"

"Sure. Why not?"

He poured her a cup of coffee and she took it, letting the steam caress her face. It smelled wonderful. She liked a strong cup of coffee, and Rey had gotten it just right. "I always liked it when you made breakfast, but you never seemed to have time."

"I have plenty of time now." He deposited a plateful of pancakes on the table. Sitting down, she eyed them curiously.

"They aren't round."

He shrugged. "They were supposed to be shaped like hearts, but it didn't go so well." They looked more like stomachs, or livers, he thought. Not very romantic.

But her smile told him she was touched, anyway. "That's very sweet."

With his own loaded plate, Rey took a seat next to her at the table and picked up the bottle of syrup. "I've got an idea for tonight."

"What's that?" She sampled a forkful of pancakes and hummed, closing her eyes as if it were an erotic experience. "These are good."

Rey squirmed a little. He'd never gotten aroused over pancakes before. It took him a second to remember what he'd been talking about. A small drop of syrup on Joely's lower lip had captured his attention. He should lean over and lick it off...

"What about tonight?" she prodded.

He dragged his attention back. His brain had gotten her naked on the kitchen table in a matter of seconds. Why was she still sitting in front of him with her clothes on? Oh, right, because this was reality. "I thought I might call Virginia and see if she has a room free for tonight. We could have sort of a mini-vacation."

She nodded reflectively. "I've always kind of wanted to stay there."

"Great. I'll make the arrangements."

"What about tomorrow, though? Perry'll need help."

"I'll take care of it." He leaned forward, catching that annoying bit of syrup with his lips. "Just leave it all up to me."

She smiled. "Okay. I'll do that. See if you can get the Romance Room."

"I will." Although he couldn't help but wonder what exactly Virginia's idea of a Romance Room might be.

• • •

Joely found herself daydreaming on her way to work. It was nice to be romanced, but she knew the novelty would wear off eventually. She also knew the difference between being courted by Rey and being married to him. The latter hadn't been such a bad deal, when their marriage had been a priority.

And he was ready to make it a priority again. He'd proven that, she thought, by coming all this way to put things right. He'd gone to a great deal of effort and seemed willing to do whatever it took to make things work. The least she could do was give him a chance.

She was ready, she thought as she pulled into a parking space in front of the boutique. Ready to take the plunge, to see where it took them.

Ready to be his wife again.

The thought brought tears to her eyes. She brushed them away as she walked into the shop. She hadn't realized, when he'd shown up here a week ago, how much she truly wanted him back in her life.

It occurred to her, looking around at the shelves of pottery, jewelry and knick-knacks, that she *could* give this up. If it came down to it, she, too, would be willing to sacrifice her job to reclaim her marriage.

She would tell him that tonight. She would tell him that, and she would tell him how much she loved him, how much she wanted to be able to wake up in bed next to him every morning for the rest of her life.

Smiling through tears of happiness, she went to the cash register and started preparations for her day.

• • •

Rey popped in just before lunch with a smile on his face. He approached Joely and dropped a kiss on her mouth, casually, as if they'd been married for years. A quick thrill ran through her, the same kind of thrill his touch always evoked in her, even a touch suitable for public consumption.

"Having a good day?" he asked. His fingers trailed down her back as he stepped away.

"So far." Out of the corner of her eye, she could see Perry's grin. "You?"

"I chatted with Virginia on the phone this morning. She asked me to come down and look at rooms so I could pick one out. So I'm headed over there."

"Get something nice," said Perry.

He winked at her. "Don't worry. I will. Can I bring you two back some lunch?"

"Of course," said Perry.

"All right. I'll be back in a bit, then." He kissed Joely again. "I'd take you with me but I want the room to be a surprise."

She watched him go. She never got tired of watching his retreating rear.

"Looking good," said Perry.

Joely cocked an eyebrow at her. "You can stop leering at my husband any time now."

Perry laughed. "I didn't mean that. I meant the whole progress of the relationship thing."

"Yes, I'd have to say progress is good."

"And you called him your husband. That's a good sign."

Surprised, Joely realized she had, indeed, referred to Rey as her husband. "You're right."

"And he does look fine in a pair of Levi's." Perry's smile had gone wicked. Joely rolled her eyes, but made no effort to argue.

• • •

The afternoon flew by, as Joely found herself thinking far too much about what awaited her this evening. What kind of room would he pick for them? She knew Virginia's lodge had a variety of eccentrically decorated rooms, but she'd never actually seen any of them other than the one where Rey had stayed his first night here. What else did he have planned?

Holding down the fort while Perry took a break, Joely leaned on the counter and settled her chin onto one hand. She pictured herself reclining on a pink-quilted bed in a sumptuously decorated room, pink roses spilling from vases on the chest of drawers, while Rey poured champagne into a glass and lifted it in a toast.

To us, he would say, and then she would tell him what she'd decided. *I don't need a month,* she would tell him. *I'm ready to take you back now, for better or for worse, forever.*

And she would kiss him then, and, champagne forgotten, they would roll back into the pretty pink bed—

"I can't believe this. Who do these people think they're fooling?"

The mocking, female voice cut through Joely's dreamy thoughts, and she lifted her head. A pair of women stood next to one of her displays of clay pottery. It was an older set, one she'd designed about eight months ago. Only a few of the pieces were left. The taller of the two women held a candy dish upside down, looking at the marks on the bottom.

"Just as I thought," the woman went on. "Taking complete credit." She set the dish back down with a clunk that made Joely wince. "All these others are just knockoffs, as well."

Joely straightened, resisting the urge to demand what the woman was blathering about. Those pieces most certainly were not knockoffs—she'd designed them herself and created them with her own sweat and tears.

The other woman posed the question, though more tactfully than Joely would have. "What makes you so sure they're knockoffs? They look like nice pieces."

The first woman snorted. "I saw these exact pieces at a boutique in Soho before we left for Vail. These podunk designers think they can get away with stealing designs from more established artists because out here in the middle of nowhere, who's going to know?" She waved dismissively at Joely's heartfelt work. "I wouldn't waste a penny on these."

A boutique in Soho. Joely swallowed, a horrible thought rising in the back of her mind. She didn't have time to work out all the implications, but she knew they were bad. Very bad.

"Excuse me, ma'am," she said.

The more abrasive of the two women jumped, as if only then becoming aware of Joely's presence.

"I'm sorry?" she said.

"You said you saw these pieces in New York. Could you tell me who the manufacturer was?"

The woman looked affronted. "I was having a private conversation with my friend."

If you wanted to have a private conversation, maybe you shouldn't have been shouting, you annoying woman. Out loud, Joely just said, "I'm sorry. I didn't mean to eavesdrop. But you can understand that I'd want to know if one of my artisans was stealing ideas. I could get into some legal trouble, and I certainly don't want that." Her voice, to her surprise, sounded not only level, but civil and accommodating.

The woman seemed placated. "They were at a boutique in Soho. But I'm certain you heard that part." She sniffed and paused. Joely got the feeling she was waiting for another apology. She wasn't going to get one. "I believe," the woman finally went on, "the manufacturer was Cherokee Ceramics."

Joely's stomach went cold. This was worse than she'd thought. "I used to work for Cherokee Ceramics."

The woman raked her with a glare. "Then I would suggest you have a talk with whatever artisan is now blatantly stealing from your former employer."

"I made those pots," Joely said, her voice cold. "And I most certainly did not steal the designs from those misogynistic, arrogant bastards at Cherokee."

The woman's eyes widened. Her companion grasped her by the elbow. "I think we should go."

"I don't think so. I want an apology."

But Joely had been pushed past her limit. "If anyone in this store is going to apologize, it's going to be you, to me. Otherwise, I suggest you leave. Now."

Haughtily, the woman gathered herself and stalked out of the store. Her companion followed, mouthing, "Sorry," over her shoulder.

Joely barely registered that they'd left. She stood stiff, shaking, her fists clenched against the counter. How was this possible? She'd parted company with Cherokee long before she'd designed that set of pots. How could they have possibly seen them?

The door to the office opened and closed behind her. Perry breezed back into the front room, then stopped.

"Joely. What's up?"

She turned toward Perry. Her face was cold, her emotions swinging wildly from anger to despair to rage. "I'm not sure yet. Something bad."

"Tell me."

Joely nodded. She told Perry about the woman's accusations, but in the middle of the story, she suddenly stopped.

Because suddenly she knew the question. The question that had nagged at her ever since Rey had arrived, but which she'd somehow been unable to put words to.

"What?" said Perry.

"Rey," Joely whispered, barely able to vocalize the thought. "This is too much of a coincidence."

"I don't get it."

Joely's fist clenched on the counter. "It's been bugging me this whole time. Why did he come? What brought him out here in the first place? Did he really ditch his whole life just to come here and declare his love?"

"Joely, no—"

"He has something to do with this. I'm sure. And I'm going to find out what."

She spun, heading toward the door. Perry caught her by the arm. "Joely, wait a minute."

Reflexively, Joely jerked her arm free from Perry's grasp. "What? Wait for what?"

"Whatever this is, and whatever it might have to do with Rey, you might not want to know."

Joely shook her head. "No. This is too important. If he's holding something back from me, I need to find out what it is."

She grabbed her coat and half ran out of the shop.

She should have known it was all too good to be true.

• • •

Her first instinct was to confront Rey directly, but she stopped abruptly on the steps leading to the front door of the lodge. If she found another way to find out what was going on, she could avoid a direct confrontation if Rey turned out not to be hiding anything. For a moment she stood there, one foot on the top step, chewing her lip. Then she turned and went back to the shop.

Perry looked up hopefully as Joely stormed back in.

"Change your mind?"

"Nope," said Joely. She stalked into the office and slammed the door behind her.

Part of her wondered what the hell she was doing. Why ruin something that was going along so well? But, leafing frantically through her old address book, she knew the answer. She had to know the truth.

By the time she found the number she was looking for, she had calmed slightly, but not enough to deter her from her purpose. Closing her eyes, she took a long, slow breath. When she could no longer feel her heartbeat slamming in the back of her throat, she picked up the phone.

"Beckford and Taylor," said the voice on the other end. "Corporate Law. This is Lisette. May I help you?"

Joely took another breath, surprise to discover she was on the verge of hyperventilating. "Is Bill Beckford in?"

"He's not available at the moment. May I take a message?"

Joely squeezed the bridge of her nose between her thumb and first finger. "Tell him Joely Birch called. I need to ask him some questions."

There was a pause on the other line. Joely assumed the receptionist was writing down the message, but then the woman said hesitantly. "Is this about Rey?"

Surprised, Joely lowered her hand. "I'm sorry. What did you say your name was again?"

"Lisette. Look, Ms. Birch, I don't know what made you decide to call, but please don't jump to conclusions."

"Don't jump to conclusions. Maybe you can answer my question, then. Did he or did he not come out to Colorado on a case?"

The pause alone was incriminating. "He did, but—"

"Something to do with Cherokee Ceramics?"

"Yes, but—"

"Then that's all I really need to know." She hung up the phone.

She turned and looked out the window, at the wide valley sweeping away in front of her. She felt as if she'd just flung herself out that window and was freefalling toward the ground, uncontrolled, with no hope of rescue or aid. Part of her wanted to scream and weep, to wail and tear her clothes, or dump ashes on her head. The rest had contracted inside her, forming a small, cold, hard ball where her heart had been.

Now she knew the answer. She knew why Rey had come out here. It hadn't been because he'd suddenly realized how much he loved and missed her. It had been work.

So what did she do now? She had no idea. She put her face in her hands, pressed the heels of her hands against her dry eyes, and sat very, very still.

• • •

Rey rubbed his hands together and surveyed the small room with a smile. Everything was perfect. The room he'd picked out for them at the lodge was appointed in lavender and dove gray. A delicate tracery of violets adorned the wallpaper, echoed in the pattern on the quilt. Or maybe it was a duvet. He wasn't sure what the difference was, but this one was delicate and pretty and seemed like it should be called something more sophisticated than a quilt.

Virginia had been more than happy to help him in his quest for a romantic room. In fact, she'd bumped a honeymooning couple from this room to another one. "They're not coming in until tomorrow. And if you're not gone by then, well, they're young. They'll recover. And the other room's nice. It's just not Joely."

This room, Rey had to admit, was very much Joely. Something about the color combinations had made him think of her the minute Virginia had waved him through the door. And on the chest of drawers sat two decorative vases and a bowl full of potpourri. Rey had thought the style looked familiar, and when he turned them over, he hadn't been surprised to find Joely's initials scratched into the bottoms.

Dinner was meticulously planned. The lodge didn't offer room service, but he'd arranged for the diner to deliver a gourmet meal, which Virginia would have one of her staff bring up. It had cost him a bit, but it would be worth it to see Joely happy.

He stepped out onto the room's small balcony, breathing the fresh mountain air and absorbing the scenery. Though it was still technically dusk, the sun was no longer visible, having dipped behind the mountains. The reddish light of the sunset combined with a medium cover of cloud to lend an orange tint to everything. Rey had never seen anything quite like it. It was beautiful and surreal, as if a giant, cold flame had engulfed the earth. He shivered a little, not sure why. The breeze that had touched his face wasn't quite cold, and the shiver had gone deeper than his skin.

Behind him, he heard the door to the room open. He didn't have to look to know it was Joely. Turning around, he met her with his brightest, most content smile.

She didn't smile back. Her face was drawn and pale. The last time she'd looked like this was the day she'd walked out on him.

His smile faded. "Joely, what's wrong?"

She pointed at a chair. "Sit, Rey. You need to answer some questions."

Rey opened his mouth to protest, but nothing came out. So he did as she'd said and sat in the chair. She loomed in front of him, arms crossed over her chest, blue eyes smoldering.

"Why are you here, Rey?" Her voice shook. He stared at her, not sure he'd heard her correctly.

"I'm sorry, Joely, I don't understand."

Her hand jerked, as if it intended to grab him by his collar, but it clenched into a fist before it reached him and lowered again. "Why did you come to Colorado? Don't lie to me. I know it wasn't just to see me."

He swallowed. How the hell had she found out? There'd been no reason for her to suspect anything.

Apparently, his silence had gone on too long, because she broke it. "I had some customers today who told me Cherokee Ceramics is selling pieces that look exactly like mine. Pieces I made after I left the company. What's the deal, Rey?"

He'd learned a long time ago to shut off his emotions in court. This wasn't court, but it was an interrogation, and the switch flicked without any conscious effort on his part. He stood, taking on a calm, professional demeanor. "Cherokee's in a great deal of trouble. There are several complaints against them right now—fourteen, I believe, at last count. I've been gathering evidence from several different artisans." He paused, took a long breath, and sealed his own fate. "Yes, I came out here to get evidence from you."

"Then why the hell didn't you just tell me that?"

He shook his head. "It didn't seem like the best way to tell you I still loved you."

Tears had gathered at the corners of her eyes. "You are an idiot, Rey."

"Yes, I am. I thought I'd gotten over that, but apparently not."

He'd hoped she might laugh, if only a little. But the corners of her mouth tightened, curling down against a sob. "I thought we had a chance."

"We do, Joely—"

"Don't, Rey. Just don't." She squeezed her eyes shut and a tear slid down her face while she shuddered, fighting the rest of them.

"Joely—" he ventured.

"No." Her emotions reined in again, her eyes opened and flashed fire into his face. "No. Don't you understand? You told me you changed, but you haven't changed. You left me because of your job, and now you're coming back because of your job."

"You left me, Joely—"

"You know what I mean. Your heart and your mind and everything that counted were gone from that house a long time before I walked out."

He took a step forward; she stepped back, her body so shaky, so unsteady, she could barely balance on her tiny, half-inch heels.

"No," she said again. "Rey, if it hadn't been for this case, would you be here right now? If I hadn't been shoved right in your face along with Cherokee Ceramics, would you have even bothered to come to Colorado?"

"Does it matter?"

"Yes, dammit, Rey, it does." She took another step back. "You're still letting your life be dictated by your job." She shook her head helplessly. "If it had been any other reason. Hell, a last-minute ski vacation would have been easier to take than this."

Desperate, he played the only card he had left. "Joely, I love you."

But she just shook her head. "I don't doubt that, Rey."

"Then what's the problem?"

"The problem is that I can't trust it. I can't trust it to be enough to hold us together."

"Why not?"

"Because it wasn't enough to bring you back."

He threw up his hands. He couldn't think of anything else to say. Hell, if "I love you" didn't work, what would?

She wheeled and grabbed the doorknob, then stopped. "Oh. One more question. Why the hell does this Lisette person know more than I do about this?"

This couldn't possibly get any worse. There was no way he could explain Lisette's involvement without making Joely even angrier than she was. It was too complicated, and he could tell Joely was in no mood to really listen to him. He shook his head against the cold anger filling his chest.

With his voice under tight control, he said, "Is there any point in trying to explain? Is there anything I could say that would change your mind?"

She lifted her chin, her expression hard, but her lips trembled. "No. No, I don't think there is."

Helpless, he watched her walk out of his life. Again.

Chapter Eleven

The next several days went by in a blur, as Joely tried to put her life back together. She should have known this would happen. It had been too much to expect that Rey could just drop back into her life and they'd automatically find a way to fix everything they'd broken the first time around. There were times when high expectations just set you up for a fall.

She found herself trapped between wanting to forget all about him and deliberately bringing his presence back. The ideas and notes he'd left behind for expanding her business were too important, she felt, to ignore. But looking at pages of his handwriting made her heart hurt.

"Just put this aside for a while," Perry told her one night, a week after Rey had left. "It can wait until it's not so hard for you."

"It's not hard," Joely snapped, and then refused to meet Perry's gaze because Perry, of course, was right.

She walked into her house at night and it was empty. It had always been empty—what was the difference? She kept telling herself that everything was the same as it had been before Rey had appeared in the shop, but it was hard to internalize that. Yes, she still had her job, her little cabin, and everything she'd had just two weeks ago. But Rey had filled all the empty spots for a while, and now they were all the emptier for his absence.

She couldn't seem to bring herself to talk to anyone about it, either. Not even Perry. Every time she tried to form words, they stopped somewhere in the back of her throat. She couldn't even cry over it. There was just nothing inside her willing to come out.

So she went to work, came home, went to sleep, woke up, went to work again. Every day. Sometimes she turned on the TV, but nothing she watched stayed in her memory for very long. Every day seemed identical to the day before. Every day was exactly the same as every day had been before Rey, but with one vital difference. All the joy had been sucked out of it.

Two weeks after Rey's ignominious departure, she sat looking at the spreadsheets again, at the rising bar graph and the profit charts. They were better even than they'd been at the end of October, but the light, heady joy she'd felt then was gone.

She shut the computer down and stared out the window. Snow filled the highest branches of the trees, weighing down the pine branches. The mountainside looked like a Christmas card. Everywhere around here looked like a Christmas card when it snowed. Nothing special about that.

Nothing special, to tell the truth, about anything anymore.

The door opened behind her and Perry came in, a worried expression on her face.

"Betty next door says you need St. John's Wort," she said.

Joely shook her head. "Prozac, more like. Or maybe a lobotomy." She sighed, surprised to feel a little of her old sense of humor coming back. "Maybe I could hire a hit man to get rid of Rey. That would make me feel better."

Perry didn't laugh. She just shook her head. "Go home, hon. Eat some tofu."

"Tofu?"

"Betty says if she knows you, you've been chocolate binging. She says you need protein."

"How does Betty know so damn much?"

"Betty's smart."

Joely had no desire to argue. She just didn't have the energy. "Okay. I'll go home. I'm not making any promises about the tofu."

When Perry had left the room, she scooped the handful of miniature Hershey's wrappers out of her drawer and stuffed them in her purse. No sense leaving evidence for Perry to show Betty.

At home, she didn't notice the blinking answering machine for a few minutes. Nobody ever called her, so she rarely paid much attention to it. Tossing a tofu-less but protein-heavy TV dinner into the microwave, she finally spotted the blinking light and frowned. Surely Rey hadn't called.

She pushed the button. A vaguely familiar woman's voice came from the machine.

"Ms. Birch, this is Lisette, Rey's secretary. I'm sure you don't want to hear from me right now, but this really has to stop. I'm getting tired of seeing Rey mope around the office, and I think Bill's about to fire him. Could you please call me back? I'll give you my home number so you can talk to me this evening if you want." She left a Manhattan number Joely didn't recognize. "As soon as possible. Please. We're dying here, I'm telling you."

The exaggerated exasperation in Lisette's voice almost made Joely laugh. Then wicked satisfaction began to seep through her. It was a strange sensation, since she'd felt so very little over the past week. So Rey was in pain, too.

Good. He deserved it.

She finished her dinner and watched the news as far as the weather before she picked up the phone.

To her surprise, something that felt like panic clawed its way up into her throat. She only managed to dial the first four numbers before she jerkily turned the handset back off.

"What the hell are you scared of, Joely?" she muttered. But there was no point asking, because she knew. Exactly the same thing she'd been scared of two weeks ago when she'd so recklessly let Rey back into her life. That he would hurt her again. Except now, he'd actually done that.

Fool me once, shame on you. Fool me twice...

She turned the TV back on and pretended to care about last night's Broncos game.

But the next night when she came home, she was almost disappointed not to see the answering machine blinking again. She ate her dinner—more protein, since it had seemed to help, but still no tofu—watched the news, then replayed last night's message.

"I think Bill's about to fire him. We're dying here, I'm telling you." Both phrases made her smile, but this time the smile didn't feel so smug.

Rey was in danger of losing his job over her. Wasn't that what he'd said he'd be willing to do? Except now it was out of mourning rather than celebration. Her smile faded. She'd been willing to give up her career, as well, hadn't she? For about five minutes there, before everything had gone haywire?

Closing her eyes, she let herself do the one thing she hadn't allowed herself to do since she'd walked out on Rey at the lodge. She thought about him.

Not just about him in general. About the way his fingers felt, trailing over her skin. The way his mouth fit against hers. His tongue tracing her breasts. The sweet slide of his body entering hers. The way her heart had expanded, warmed, pounded, as she looked up into his desire-darkened eyes. The sounds, the smell, the touch of him. The warmth of him asleep in bed beside her.

Tears gathered in her eyes. She picked up the phone and dialed Lisette's home number.

"Lisette?" she said to the other woman's "Hello."

"Yes."

"This is Joely Birch."

"Joely, I'm so glad to hear from you—"

"Lisette," Joely broke in. "I'm sorry, Lisette. I can't do it. Tell Rey if you have to. I just can't do it."

Uncertain of her own resolve, she hung up before Lisette could protest.

• • •

It got better after a while. By Thanksgiving, Joely felt like she'd fallen back into her old patterns. She ate turkey and played Trivial Pursuit at Perry's house, then, back home, spent an hour on the phone with her mother, talking about anything but Rey. The world started to look friendly again.

Which was, of course, when it happened.

Wednesdays were usually quiet at the shop, even this close to Christmas, so Joely was surprised when Perry came fluttering into the office, looking frantic. Assuming a crowd of customers had just arrived, Joely said, "I'll be right there."

"No, Joely," said Perry. Her voice squeaked strangely. "It's him again. It's Rey."

Joely stared at her. "You have *got* to be kidding."

"No way. I'd recognize that ass anywhere."

Joely straightened the papers on her desk, then wondered why she'd done it. Thinking only marginally more clearly, she stood, straightened her hair, and went for the door. With her hand gripping the knob, she threw a last, desperate look back at Perry.

"Go!" said Perry. "Kill the man if you have to, but *go!*"

Joely went.

It was déjà vu all over again. Rey stood next to the display of wolf-themed pots—only two of which had sold since his first appearance—only this time he wore jeans and a New York Rangers sweatshirt instead of an Armani suit. He looked better in the jeans.

"Rey," she said, frustrated by the tremble in her voice.

He turned. His normally neat hair had grown a little too long, just enough to make him look unkempt. He looked tired, and carried a thick manila envelope in one hand.

"This altitude's a bitch," he said with a pained smile.

She only chewed her lip, trying hard not to remember the effect the altitude had had on him before, how he'd slept there in front of her, his face soft and quiet as a little boy's.

He gave a helpless shrug. "I guess you don't want to talk to me. I don't blame you." He lifted the envelope. "There are some things in here for you to look at. About the lawsuit against Cherokee, and some other things. I'm staying downtown. Give me a call when you've signed everything."

She took the envelope. "You could have mailed these. You didn't have to come all the way out here."

The pain in his eyes made her flinch. "Yes, I did." He took a step backward, toward the door. He smiled a little but the pain hadn't changed. Joely blinked and swallowed. She refused to cry in front of him. Or behind him, as he turned toward the door. Or about him, as the door closed behind him.

She stood still for far too long, staring at the closed door, before she heard the creak of hinges behind her.

"Joely?" came Perry's hesitant voice. "Is he gone?"

Joely nodded, coming back to herself. "He's gone."

She walked back behind the counter and headed into the office. The tears had faded and she felt stable again, but her hands still shook as she drew a pile of legal papers out of the long envelope.

"What is it?" Perry asked.

Joely looked up to see her friend watching around the edge of the door. "I don't know. Something to do with the suit against Cherokee Ceramics, he said." But another set of papers fluttered out, papers she recognized. She swallowed, staring at them as they drifted to the floor.

The divorce papers. With his signature scrawled across the bottom.

Her face must have gone as bleak as her heart, because Perry said, "Do you want me to stay?"

"Yeah. Maybe."

Perry propped the door open so they could hear the bell on the front door, then took a seat across from Joely at the desk. She picked up the divorce papers and held them tentatively out to Joely.

"Just lay them down," Joely said. "I'll look at that later."

Forcing her gaze away from the divorce papers, she focused her attention on the rest of the envelope's contents. On top were documents pertaining to a class action lawsuit against Cherokee Ceramics. She glanced over them.

"Oh, my God."

"What?" said Perry.

"They've agreed to settle out of court. All I have to do is sign some papers and I'll get a cash reimbursement."

"How much?"

Joely showed Perry the sum.

"Wow. That'll pay the rent for a while."

"It certainly will."

Joely gave the figure one last, unbelieving look, then went to the next document. She couldn't imagine what else he might have for her.

She read the next sheet, but at first it didn't make any sense. She held it out to Perry. "Is this what I think it is?"

Perry looked perplexed, as well. "It's a letter of resignation. Rey quit his job?"

"Why would he do that?" She flipped through the remaining papers, searching for an explanation. The next stack was more pertaining to the lawsuit, but under that was a sheet of blue-lined notebook paper, filled with Rey's neat, thin handwriting. Tears sprang to Joely's eyes. She dashed them away in irritation. She didn't want to cry. Not over him. Not again.

"Read it?" Perry asked, but Joely shook her head. She needed Perry's emotional support, but she was afraid if she read the letter aloud she'd be in tears after a matter of words.

Joely, the letter began. *As you can see, I've quit my job. If you don't believe I'm serious now, you never will. I want to work this out. We need to talk. Call me at my hotel.* A downtown number followed. *If you truly think there's no hope, I've signed the papers so you can file them.*

"Not much here, after all," she mumbled, handing the letter to Perry. She added the divorce papers neatly to the rest of the envelope's contents and slid everything else back into the envelope. "I don't want to talk to him," she said firmly.

Perry tilted an eyebrow at her over the top of the letter. "You're sure about that?"

"No."

When Rey had been standing there in the shop, she'd wanted more than anything else to touch him. To slip her fingers through his untidy hair, to slide her hands under his shirt. She'd never had that kind of chemistry with another man, and doubted she ever would. A life without Rey would mean a life without something unutterably precious.

But so, so painful if it didn't work.

"What are you going to do?" Perry finally said softly into the silence.

Joely scrubbed her forehead. "I don't know." She managed a weak smile. "I'll keep you posted."

Perry's return smile was a little sad. She squeezed Joely's hand. "Whatever you decide, I'll be here."

"Thanks."

• • •

She went home, ate dinner, watched the weather. It seemed to be a necessary ritual before making a decision. Finally, still unsure whether it was supposed to snow tomorrow, she picked up the phone.

"Okay," she said to Rey when he answered. "Let's talk. When can you come up?"

"I'm not coming up." His voice was taut. "You come here."

His insistence took her aback. "Why?"

"I'll explain when you get here."

She chewed her lip. "Okay. Fine." She looked at the clock. "I can come down tonight."

"Great." His voice had relaxed a little. "Have you had dinner?"

"Yes."

"Then I guess you can just meet me at the hotel."

"Okay. It's going to take me at least an hour and a half."

"Take your time. I don't want you to hurt yourself."

This touched her for some reason. With his voice going furry around the words, it sounded like he really meant it. Her own voice sounded furry when she spoke again, though for different reasons. "Okay. I'll see you in a bit."

The ride down the mountain was surreal. In the darkness and occasionally light traffic, there were times when it seemed hers was the only car on the highway, flying over the hills and through the wide curves like a roller coaster in the dark.

Closer to town, the traffic increased. She found herself watching the cars rush by, wondering if anyone else was in as much turmoil as she was. Where were they going? Meeting a lover for an illicit affair? Taking a child to the hospital? Even going home after a long day's work had its own drama. Every car held its own story. Hers was, perhaps, no more dramatic than any of the others.

She tightened her hands on the steering wheel at the thought. Other people had been through this kind of thing and had survived. People even now, possibly in that blue Dodge that had just moved into her lane, were going through even worse. Whatever happened, she would get through it.

By the time she pulled into the parking lot of Rey's hotel, she was calmer again. She picked up the envelope full of papers, slung her purse over her shoulder, and walked firmly up to the front door.

Rey sat in the lobby. Sighting her, he stood and smiled softly. All her calm control wavered and she clenched her teeth in a desperate attempt to hang onto it. Keeping her stride firm, she crossed the room to him, noting with some irritation that he hadn't bothered to move at all. The irritation rose until she wasn't sure if she was scared, apprehensive, or just plain mad.

"Let's go upstairs, shall we?" He made an inviting gesture toward the elevators.

Not trusting herself to say anything, Joely headed in the direction he indicated. In silence, they rode the elevator up, walked down the hallway to Rey's room.

By the time he closed the door behind them, Joely had sorted through her emotions and decided she was, indeed, angry.

"This is nice, Rey," she grated. "Drag me all the way down the mountain and don't even talk to me."

He regarded her calmly. "Did you read the papers?"

"Yes."

"All of them?"

"Yes."

Nodding, he crossed to the bed and sat on it. She stood in front of him, clutching the envelope.

"Since you drove down here," he went on, "I assume you didn't go ahead and sign the divorce papers?"

"No, I didn't."

He nodded again. She watched, perplexed, as he lifted another legal-sized manila envelope from the nightstand. "Good. Then I have another proposal." He held the envelope out to her. "You might want to take a look at this."

Joely didn't want to take a look at anything. Flinging her envelope onto the bed, she planted her fists against her hips. "No, I don't think I do. What is this, Rey?"

"It's a pre-re-nup, I guess."

She gaped. "You want to get back together but you want to put conditions on it?"

"You could say that."

So angry she couldn't even speak, she instead growled the emotion and spun, stalked two steps toward the door.

"Joely, I love you."

That stopped her. Why, she wasn't sure. It wasn't as if he hadn't said it before. Hearing it now didn't make any of the rest of their situation go away. But something in his tone touched her. He sounded calm, but at the same time wounded.

Slowly, she turned back around. "And? Or is it 'But'?"

"But I can't go through this again. And I can't take the blame for everything that goes wrong. Even when it doesn't."

"I don't understand."

He pushed his envelope toward her. "Read it."

For the moment, curiosity overcame irritation. She took the envelope and drew out its contents.

It was a legal document, three pages long. From what little she knew about the subject, it contained all the elements of a prenuptial agreement, but when she got to the body of the document, things began to change.

"I, Reynard Birch," she read aloud, "hereby affirm that I will not focus my attention so thoroughly on my job that I forget about my marriage." She gave him a narrow look. "That sounds all right."

"Keep reading."

She cleared her throat, looking for the place where she'd left off. "I, Joely Birch, hereby affirm that I will accept all communications with Reynard Birch in the spirit in which they were intended, regardless of whether they conform to my preconceived notions." Okay, this wasn't so nice. "Excuse me?"

Rey's smile had faded. "I meant every word I said to you. Who cares if Lisette had to kick me in the ass to get the process started? My head was so far up there she damn near broke my nose."

Joely shook her head. "All you were thinking about was the case."

He took a jerky step toward her, his body taut. With anger, frustration or desire, Joely couldn't tell. "No. The case brought my attention back around where it should have been all along. To you. It's a damn shame I ever let it drift that far. I regret that. I'm sorry for that. But if we're going to have half a hope in hell of making this work, you can't hold it over my head every chance you get."

She didn't know what to say. Was that what she'd been doing? In the guise of protecting her heart, had she laid the blame for everything that had gone wrong in their marriage squarely at Rey's feet?

She had. But right now she wasn't quite so sure it all belonged there.

She swallowed and straightened her spine. Time to face facts. "Go on."

"There's more in there, about what constitutes infidelity, and the consequences of lying. We never had any problem with that, though."

"Just your affair with your job."

"Yeah. I think we covered that, though." He fiddled his fingers in the air. "Flip to the last page."

She did. Reading it, she wasn't sure if it was appropriate to laugh, but she did anyway. "Rey, this is nuts."

"Just read it. Tell me what you think."

"'In the event of any perceived or actual breach of the above agreements, in part or in full, the involved parties agree to abide by the following procedure to settle this breach.' Rey! A *procedure?*"

"It seemed prudent under the circumstances. Read on."

She scanned the page. "Rey, I really don't think it's possible or even wise to make love during the course of an argument."

He arched a brow, a challenge in his eyes. "Why?"

"Well…wouldn't you forget what you were arguing about?"

"That's the point. Now, read the last two items and then we can decide if we want to proceed."

"Okay. 'I, Joely Birch, hereby agree to give Reynard Birch the benefit of the doubt in any and all situations. I, Reynard Birch, hereby agree to give Joely Birch top priority in any and all situations, including those related to advancement of career.' You already signed yours."

"I did."

She still didn't quite know what to think. "Is this a legally binding document?"

"Probably not."

"Then why did you do it?"

He shrugged. "I'm a lawyer. I think better this way. Besides, it doesn't have to be legally binding to make us think about what we're doing before it all blows to hell again."

She nodded. Frowning, she read the last few paragraphs again. "Rey," she finally said, slowly. "I don't know if this is the most romantic thing I've ever seen or the most offensive."

He looked surprised. "There's no in between?"

"I'm not really seeing one."

Doubt crept into his face. Good. Maybe he was figuring out that the best way to a woman's heart wasn't through legal documents.

"Maybe you could go for the former?" he said hopefully.

She shook her head. Frustration warred with need. Why couldn't he get it? "I don't know. This is a whole new wrinkle, Rey. I'm going to have to think about it."

Frustration won. She tossed the folder onto the bed and left.

Chapter Twelve

"How dare he?" Joely muttered to herself as she shoved a finger into the elevator call button. Rey's whole plan for reconciliation seemed to revolve around shifting the blame to her. What kind of nonsense was that?

How can he say any of this was my fault? He's the one who got so wrapped up in his job there was no time for me.

You're *the one who walked out.*

The thought prodded at her, making her angrier. She stomped into the elevator and shoved the button for the lobby.

"I had a reason to walk out," she muttered, mostly under her breath but still loud enough that the other person on the elevator took a wary step away from her. Joely gave him a wan smile that she hoped didn't make her look like an axe murderer.

He didn't seem greatly reassured. She kept her fuming to herself until they reached the lobby and he made a hasty retreat.

Joely had had every intention of heading back up the mountain. But on her way to the parking lot, her feet slowed, and finally stopped. Something didn't feel right. Something in the back of her mind kept nudging her. Something in her heart felt askew.

Grudgingly, she admitted she couldn't go any farther without figuring out what that something was. She turned around and headed back to the lobby, to the restaurant. She could sit for a while with a drink or some nachos and think.

But she didn't make it to the restaurant, either. Just outside the door, her feet stopped again.

Thinking wasn't going to do her any good. She needed to make a phone call.

• • •

Rey let himself fall backwards onto the bed. He'd thought he had things figured out, but it had all gone hellishly wrong.

The re-nup was supposed to have made her laugh. It had been the best way he could think of to air his grievances without having the situation spiral into an argument. It had spiraled anyway, and she'd walked out.

Again. So much for the third time being a charm.

He scrubbed his hands over his face. The entire venture had been doomed from the start. He should never have let Lisette talk him into it in the first place, much less the second time.

If only Joely could understand what he'd been trying to tell her. He didn't think it had been that much to ask. As far as he was concerned, the only thing standing between him and a happy life with his wife was her inability to admit she'd played a part in their breakup.

He understood her need to blame him. He'd blamed her for a long time. As their marriage had crumbled, she'd found less and less to say to him, closed more and more lines of communication. But he'd failed to use even the ones she'd left open, and when she had spoken to him he'd made little effort to listen. So, when faced with the prospect of seeing her again, he'd swallowed part of his pride and admitted to himself that he had to share the blame. She didn't seem willing to take a similar step.

She had to, though, if this was going to work. He couldn't always be the bad guy.

But, and he admitted this to himself with a wrench of pain, there wasn't a whole hell of a lot he could do about it now. It was all up to Joely.

...

Sitting in a large, comfortable chair in the lobby, Joely dialed her cell phone. It had been a long time since she'd retrieved messages from her home answering machine, and it took her three tries before she got the password right. When she did, she found Lisette's message and replayed it, jotting down the Manhattan phone number. She glanced at her watch. It would be late in New York, maybe too late for a polite phone call.

She dialed the number anyway. It had to be done.

Lisette at least sounded alert when she answered. Joely could hear the familiar voice of a late-night talk show host in the background.

"I'm sorry to bother you at this hour," said Joely. "This is Joely Birch."

The sound of the TV faded. "Hi, Joely. It's okay, I'm just watching TV. What can I do for you?"

Joely closed her eyes, gathering her nerve. "I just need to know what your part is in all this."

There was a pause on the other end. "I'm sorry, but I don't really understand why."

"It seems to me that if Rey really wanted to get back together, he would have come up with the idea himself. He wouldn't have needed any prodding from anyone else."

Lisette snorted. "He's a *man*, Ms. Birch."

True, but the answer seemed too flippant to Joely. "It leaves me with a lot of questions."

Like, exactly who are you to him? What's he not telling me that I need to know? She chewed her lip, waiting for Lisette to break the suddenly taut silence.

"Okay. I think I know what some of them are." The background TV noise disappeared altogether. "Are you absolutely sure you want to hear this, Ms. Birch?"

Joely rubbed her forehead. "It can't possibly get any worse than it already is. Just tell me. And call me Joely."

Lisette's voice embarked on a story. Joely wondered what she looked like. What kind of expression was on her face? Was she enjoying her role as dropper of bombshells? Worse, was it possible she would just introduce another impossible element to the situation by lying to Joely? Maybe Lisette wanted Rey for herself.

The story unwound.

"I dated Rey a couple of times." Okay, this was bad. Joely closed her eyes. "When we got to the third date, I tried to seduce him." This was worse. "No luck. Now, when a man passes up commitment-free sex, I know there's a problem. So the next time we went out, I got him drunk."

Joely tipped her head back against the couch. Tears teased the corners of her eyes. "Do I want to hear the rest of this?"

"Yes, you do. I still couldn't get him to sleep with me, but under the influence of Captain Morgan and José Cuervo, he told me his entire life story. Which was when I found out about you." There was a pause. "Joely, I know when I'm beat. I didn't have a chance in hell with him. And he was such a mess—he said you gave him no warning, just threw divorce papers at him and left. It blindsided him. So when the suit with Cherokee came up, I just gave him a nudge. And when he came back home two weeks ago, I gave him another one. Now, apparently, you need the treatment. So you got it. Whatever it is that's keeping you away from him, get the hell over it. You won't regret it."

Joely blinked as the tears slid down her face. She could summon no words.

After a moment Lisette said, "Are you all right?"

"No," Joely managed.

"Can I do anything else for you?"

"No." She dried her face with the back of one hand. "Thank you, Lisette. I'm sorry to have bothered you."

Before Lisette could say anything else, Joely hung up the phone.

Blindsided. How could Rey have been blindsided? Hadn't he seen how unhappy she was?

But maybe that was the point. Had she ever actually told him?

For the first time, Joely tried to put herself in Rey's place. Devastated by his defeat in the courtroom. His wife jobless because of his failure. Humiliated. Trying to redeem himself in the only way he knew how—by excelling at his job.

And then one night to come home and face Joely's anger. Anger that had built over months of frustration she hadn't expressed to him. Frustration she'd nurtured inside her, assuming he should just automatically know, as if mental telepathy were a natural side effect of love.

Then, after all that time, to come to her and shoulder blame that didn't all belong to him, only to have that thrown back into his face over something as trivial as the involvement of a friend.

Joely squeezed her eyes shut tight, trying to shut out the pain constricting her heart. "My God," she whispered. "What have I done?"

• • •

He could do one of two things, Rey decided. He could stay here and hope she came back. Or he could get in his car and chase her back up the mountain, fall at her feet and beg her to take him back.

Both choices had a certain appeal. But, technically, he'd already tried them both and neither had worked.

Maybe it was time to just let it go.

He gave a long, resigned sigh. The Joely-less chapter of his life was about to begin.

He had never felt so empty. It was as if someone had just ripped a piece of his soul out, brutally, and without benefit of anesthetic.

This was worse, even, than the day she'd walked out. Because this time he knew he'd done everything he could to mend the rifts, and nothing had worked.

He hadn't cried since he was seven, but he felt the tears now, in a big, ugly wad at the back of his throat. Ruthlessly, he swallowed them.

This wasn't going to happen.

He grabbed his car keys from the nightstand and stalked to the door.

He jerked the door open, and froze.

Joely stood in the hallway, one fist raised, ready to knock.

"Joely," he said, and she said, "Rey," in the same breath.

There was no getting over the awkwardness. He just stared at her for far too long, without realizing it was far too long. Time seemed to have stopped, hovering between them, waiting for one of them to do something so it could move again.

Finally, he took a step backward. "Come in."

She did, not looking at him or touching him. Deliberately, too, because she had to contort her body backward strangely to keep from brushing her chest against his.

He turned, watching her back as she walked into the room. "I figured you'd be halfway back up the mountain by now."

She wheeled around to face him. Her face was bleak. "I probably should be. At least that way I could keep from saying anything stupid."

"Stupid like what?"

"Stupid like I'm sorry, I love you." She shrugged. "And I'm sorry."

"That was supposed to be my line."

"That's what I thought, too. I think maybe I was wrong."

He crossed his arms over his chest, regarding her. "What do you mean?"

"I mean that for all this time, I've totally blamed you for breaking up our marriage. But maybe I had something to do with it, too."

He pressed his lips tightly together to keep from saying anything. This was a big step for her, he knew, and he didn't want to discourage her by being a jerk about it. She looked at him like she was waiting for him to say something, so he nodded. "I'm listening."

Her lips trembled and she compressed them for a moment, tears filling her eyes. He wanted to touch her, to say something, to do something, but he had no idea what she would accept right now. Finally, the shivering in her mouth stilled. She blinked a few times before she spoke.

"Did I ever, in all the time you were working so much, did I ever tell you how I felt about it?"

Slowly, he shook his head. "Did I ever ask you?"

She arched a graceful sweep of blonde eyebrow in surprise. "No. You never did." She paused, her gaze becoming a bit more shrewd. He wondered what kinds of gears were turning behind her eyes. "Did I ever tell you I felt alone?"

"No. Did I ever tell you how much it hurt, losing that case?"

"You never really talked to me about it at all."

Taking a step toward her, he nodded. Her brows compressed in puzzlement as he held both hands out to her. "Maybe we should follow the rules on this one?"

For the space of a long, held breath, he wondered if he'd just blown the whole thing. But finally she smiled, then actually laughed a little, and held out her own hands. "Maybe we should."

He closed his fingers around hers as they settled across from each other on the bed. "Don't let go," he said. "Whatever happens, just don't let go."

She nodded. "You first."

"No. You go on."

At first he thought she might protest, but she squeezed her eyes tight. Her hands tightened a little on his at the same time. After a second or two, she opened her eyes and said, "It seemed to me like you were closing me out more and more, and it didn't matter if I said anything or not, because it was like you weren't even there."

He nodded. Fair enough. "I felt like I had to redeem myself to you. I felt like I'd ruined your life because I lost you your job. It was hard for me to even face you, much less wonder if I was hurting you."

"You were hurting so much yourself."

"No, no." He gave her a crooked smile. "No comments allowed yet."

"Then what do we do next?"

"Kiss me."

"What?"

"Those are the rules. You talk, then I talk, and then you kiss me."

"Okay, I think I remember something about that."

She scooted forward on the bed, keeping her legs crossed, until her knees bumped against his. Then, still holding tight to his hands, she leaned forward and kissed him.

He closed his eyes, the better to taste and feel the press of her lips against his. He didn't want to lose this again. The kiss was gentle, almost hesitant, but soon began to simmer. He drew back just as he felt her mouth begin to slacken, ready to let him in. No need to go too fast.

"For a long time, I blamed this on you," he said, "because you were the one who left." Hurt sprang up in her eyes and her hands pulled a little away from his. He tightened his grasp on her fingers, maintaining the connection. "I didn't want to admit I'd done anything wrong." A wry smile curled his lips. "I don't think you understand how hard it is for a man to admit he's wrong."

"It was a big thing, you coming out here." Her eyes had gone moist again.

"Yes, it was. But it's your turn. No comments."

"It seemed like there was no way to get your attention. You didn't even want to make love to me anymore." She bit her lip as if trying to call back what she'd said.

But he only nodded slowly, understanding in his eyes. "I had the same feeling about you. Like you weren't interested anymore."

"But—"

"No, no. No comments yet." He shifted closer. "Now I kiss you."

She looked skeptical, but tilted her head closer to him. "Are you sure this is going to work?"

"No. I made it all up off the top of my head." He moved just a little closer, his lips nearly brushing hers. "My guess is it's all a load of crap."

He kissed her before she could respond, and she laughed against his lips. It was hard to resist the soft opening of her mouth. More than that, it was pointless. He pressed closer, letting his tongue slip past her lips.

She was right. It was hard to focus on the disagreement with these interludes. He wasn't sure if this was a good thing or a bad thing.

It felt good, though, it tasted good as he explored more deeply. Her response felt good, too, as she tugged her hands loose from his and put her arms around him, pulling him closer. Her body went warm and soft, melting between her legs. She felt safe here, in spite of everything.

He thought she was as lost in the kiss as he was, but this time she pulled back.

"Aren't we supposed to have a time limit on this part of it?"

"Something like that." He tried to dive in again but she ducked out of his way.

"Seriously, Rey. They're your rules. Are we following them, or not?"

"We should try." Reining in the intense surge of his libido, he schooled his features to studiousness. "Whose turn is it?"

"I don't remember."

"Neither do I."

"Is that bad or good?" She seemed anxious about the answer.

"I don't know. We haven't really settled anything."

He nestled her against him, sliding his hands down her back. "I don't think we need to settle everything tonight."

"What *do* we need to settle?" Her back had tensed a little under his hands.

"I'm not sure."

It was strange, she thought, how serious it had gotten so suddenly. Frightening, almost, but not quite. She wanted to plunge back into that kiss they'd started, but she wasn't sure if that was allowed by Rey's rules. On the other hand, she wasn't sure the rules were any use at all.

"We still have it," she said. "You can't deny that."

"Still have what?"

"That thing."

"What thing?"

"That thing that makes me wobbly when you kiss me. That makes me hot, and wet, and makes me want you inside me so badly, I can hardly stand it."

She wasn't sure if his smile was loving or just plain smug. But it faded before she could be sure. "Is that enough?" he asked.

"It's a start."

It would have been easy, she thought, to dive right back in. She knew what he could do to her, knew how much she wanted that. But she also knew how much it hurt to lose it.

"I think I remember what came next in the procedure," she said.

"Promises?"

"Right." She scooted a little farther back, putting more space between them. She needed it, to clear her head. "Grievances, then promises."

"You start."

After a moment of consideration, she said, "I promise to stop trying to find all the hidden meanings in what you do and don't do."

He quirked an eyebrow at that, but made no comment. Which was good, because comments weren't allowed right now. "I promise to pay more attention to what's going on with you, regardless of whether I understand it."

How had they gotten so insightful all of a sudden? Maybe their long separation had taught them something, after all. If nothing else, it had given them plenty of time to reflect on what they'd done wrong.

"Do I do another one?" she asked. She couldn't remember what the procedure had said.

"Yes, but it has to be something you want me to do."

An interesting and logical twist. Something a lawyer would come up with. "Okay…" She thought for a time, working her way past the flippant answers to something that would actually make a difference. "I would like you to promise to ask me once in a while how I'm feeling, in case I forget to tell you."

"That's good," he said, "because I want you to tell me."

"I'll try."

Reaching for her hands, he lifted them again in his. "One more thing." He cleared his throat. "'Faithful and true, I love only you, now and forever, forsaking you never.'"

The words made her want to smile and cry, made her heart feel light with joy and weighted with love. "'With your hand in mine, everything will be fine, for where there is love, God smiles from above.'"

His laugh fell like warm rain. "Whatever possessed us to write our own vows? We were terrible poets."

"But we meant them, didn't we?"

"Yes, we did."

"And I mean them again now."

Leaning toward her, he spoke against her lips. "Me, too."

But she ducked back, away from his kiss. "I'm sorry. I don't know if this is allowed. Are we still following the procedure?"

"This *is* the procedure." And he dipped his head again and kissed her so thoroughly she couldn't fight it anymore.

He slid his hands up her body, and a moment later he had rolled her backwards, pressing her down into the bed.

"This is Phase Two," he muttered into her ear. "Are we done with Phase One?"

"Stick a fork in Phase One, it's done," said Joely, and grabbed him by the hair and kissed him hard.

Phase Two, she decided, was much better than Phase One. From here on out, she was going to do everything she could to be sure they spent as much time as possible in Phase Two. It was almost worth having to go through Phase One to get here, but it would be better if they could bypass it altogether.

She pulled his shirt open, narrowly missing yanking loose a few buttons. Moments later her face was buried in his chest, her nostrils full of his smell, his soft hair tickling her face. His legs tangled with hers, his weight pressing her into the bed. She wanted him so badly, couldn't stand the thought of the layer of clothing between his skin and hers.

He was already working on that situation. His long fingers pressed loose the button on her jeans, jerked down the zipper, then slid under her panties. Too fast, she thought at first, but it wasn't. She was more than ready for him, all wetness and heat as his fingers dipped inside her. He slid two fingers in, in an easy glide, and her body opened to the penetration, ready, more than willing.

As he worked her, his fingers probing, thrusting, she clutched him hard against her, moaned against his throat, then fastened her mouth to the pulse there. She loved the taste of his skin. She devoured it, kissing up the side of his neck, lipping his earlobe.

One hand dove into his hair while the other fought to open his fly. She worked the button loose, then the zipper, her fingers plunging past to curl around his rapidly thickening shaft. It grew as she touched it, hardening within the curve of her fingers.

A moment's separation then, just enough to shimmy down his pants and hers, enough to allow skin to meet skin all down the length of her legs. The roughness of the hair on his thighs against the smoothness of hers aroused her to the point of tears.

"I love you," he murmured, a sensuous slide of his gorgeous mouth against her ear. "I love you so much."

"Never leave me again," she said.

"I won't if you won't."

"I won't." And a weight lifted from her heart, because she knew without a doubt it was the truth.

He tilted his head back just long enough for her to see the tears brimming in his eyes, then lowered his head to her breast.

Her world narrowed to the movement of his mouth, his tongue against her nipple, circling it, his teeth touching it carefully, his mouth suckling. Fire stabbed through her, breast to groin, filled her, impaled her.

He moved down, his lips soft and mobile against her belly, her navel, her thigh, tongue tracing cool trails over her skin. Then his hands gentle against the insides of her thighs. He cupped her knees, flattened his palms against them, opened her up. Bending in toward her, he kissed the soft flesh high inside her thigh, bit her gently, firmly, licked her, moved up, until his mouth closed over her.

She closed her eyes, just feeling. She was as vulnerable here as it was possible to be, but there was nothing to be afraid of. She was open to him, taken by him. His tongue slid over her and she shivered, feeling her body begin to weep for him. Then thought vanished as she rose and crested, her body shaking, her voice coming out in a keen at the intensity of her orgasm.

When she was done, as her shivering climax stilled, he lifted his head and pillowed his face against her belly. He was breathing nearly as hard as she was, caught up in her ecstasy. Her hands slid down her own skin until they touched his hair, slid into its thick silk. He looked up at her face and smiled.

"Come inside," she whispered.

His smile deepened and warmed. There was a moment's pause as he fumbled in the pocket of his cast-aside jeans for a condom, then he kissed his way back up her body. He licked her breasts, one nipple, then the other, kissed her collarbone, her throat, her mouth. Finally, hand on her thigh, he pressed her open and slid inside her.

She let out a slow, deep breath, feeling him slide in. He kissed her again, savoring her mouth before he began the rhythm. He rose above her, and feeling his movement inside her, she suddenly realized she was no longer afraid. Her heart was safe with him; she knew that now. Fear was no longer relevant.

The realization made her want to weep. The tears gathered on the edges of her lids until she could no longer fight them. He saw, and kissed her damp cheeks even as his own climax took him over. With his lips against her tears, he stilled inside her, pressing hard into her, the warm sensation spreading up into her chest. She could feel him come, could feel his body tauten, feel him pulse. Finally, he let out a ragged breath and opened his eyes. His face was wet, and she touched the tears with the tips of her fingers.

"I'm coming home with you tonight," he said. He lifted a hand, cupping her breast, stroking her nipple with his thumb. "But only on one condition."

She blinked, startled. "Condition?" She thought they'd covered everything, settled all their differences. What was he going to do now? What was he going to say that would ruin it all?

He brushed her hair back from her forehead. "Yes. Just one. Just one little one."

"What?"

"You need to turn the heat up at night."

She laughed, relieved. "God, that's all? You scared me." She touched his face, feeling the beginnings of rough stubble. "Okay, I can do that." Pulling him closer, she whispered into his ear. "But I still think heat's for wimps."

Epilogue

April in the Rockies was unpredictable, but for this day the weather had cooperated.

Standing on the ridge behind her house, just above where the backyard began its dizzying descent down into the valley, Joely shaded her eyes and peered toward the distant peaks.

"So much for that snow the weatherman predicted yesterday."

Perry grinned. "He didn't know you were getting married today."

"Oh, that's right," said Joely with a grin. "I forgot to call him."

The last few months had been wonderful. Starting life all over again with Rey was an adventure she was glad she hadn't missed out on. It had been a great deal like the first months of their marriage, way back when, but sweeter in some ways. In other ways it was bittersweet, as they thought about what they'd lost, but they tried not to dwell on that aspect of it.

Given what they'd been through, it seemed only appropriate to Joely that they commemorate this new stage in their relationship. Especially now.

"So how are you feeling this morning?" Perry asked.

"Better. I actually managed to eat a little breakfast this morning instead of just saltines."

"No barfing on the groom, now," Perry cautioned.

Joely grinned. "Why not? This is all his fault."

"Now, now, what happened to all those promises about unfair blame? Last I heard, it took two to make a baby."

Joely's eyes twinkled as she stroked her barely-rounded abdomen. It would be a while before she started to show. "Yeah, I guess I have to admit I was there."

"So when is the groom due to arrive?"

"Three. He went into work this morning to finish up some things so he won't have to worry about them while we're gone." They were honeymooning for four days near Mesa Verde. Low-key, but that was what they both wanted.

Rey had found a job, not in Denver, but at a small but well-established law firm in Evergreen. He'd taken a sizable salary cut, but the cost of living here wasn't nearly as high as in Manhattan. He seemed to enjoy it, too, once he'd adjusted to the slower pace. It was an opportunity to learn more about family law and environmental issues, and that also had proved a benefit. It seemed to Joely he was more at peace with himself and her and the entire world than he ever had been before.

And now there would be a baby. They'd need to look for a larger house—Joely's little cabin was barely big enough for herself and Rey, much less a child and all the necessary accoutrements. That, too, they'd take one step at a time.

Rey arrived home early, and at four o'clock they stood in front of a minister, reciting newly written vows.

Joely took Rey's hands in hers and looked into his dark eyes. "With the good times ahead and the bad times behind, I pledge myself to you, heart, soul, and mind."

His mouth quirked a little. She knew it was miserable poetry—she didn't care. His wouldn't be any better.

"We made our mistakes but we move on in love, for where two hearts are mended, God smiles from above."

"I pronounce you re-wed," said the minister. She, too, wore a silly grin. "What God has brought forth, let none set amiss, now seal your new love with a re-married kiss."

Joely laughed out loud. That hadn't been in the program. But Rey cut her mirth short with a firm kiss, his hand cupping her belly. After a long, gentle moment, he tilted his head back.

"You're never getting rid of me now," he said.

She tapped the end of his nose. "Good. That's the way it should be."

And there, under the April sun, with his hand against the soft curve of her abdomen, she knew it was the way it would always be.

A Sneak Peek from Crimson Romance

(From *The Wicked Bad* by Karyn Gerrard)

You can't go home again. But what did Nick Crocetti know? He'd never had a home.

One thing he could not stand was any form of rank sentiment. Especially in himself. The emotion had been missing from his tumultuous life for years, so why in hell did it rear its ugly head now?

Nick glared at the name on the colorful flyer he had pulled from under the door of his bar. Veronica Barnes Titus. *Ronnie Barnes.* The annoyingly cheerful flyer announced the grand opening of Titus Bakery on Waterloo Street.

It couldn't be her; she had left town ages ago. Titus? Right, he'd heard talk she'd married, was she still? He hoped the rumors of her recent divorce were true. Any talk of Ronnie Barnes perked his interest through the years, though he would outwardly pretend he didn't give a damn what she'd been up to.

Nick crossed the threshold and closed the door behind him. He tossed his keys on the bar and hit the light switch by the door. Fluorescent lights flickered and buzzed washing the brick interior in a hazy illumination.

He spread the flyer out on the counter and read it again. When he saw her last at her father's funeral, he'd kept a respectable distance. She was still the luscious blonde he remembered and she still wore glasses that always seemed to slide down her nose. It's not as if they'd ever spoken to each other. Nick knew her brother Tyler slightly, they were the same age. He should've walked up to her and offered his condolences, but she no doubt would've seen the blatant lust in his eyes. A crass statement at a funeral, especially her father's.

The memories roared back whether he wanted them to or not. Nick arrived in Rockland, Maryland in the twelfth grade. At the time, he had nowhere else to go, so he lived with his uncle, a man he barely knew because his parents had washed their hands of him. Nick's home had never been a happy one, and with his parents obtaining a divorce and going their separate ways, neither wanted a hulking six-footer who hadn't finished growing and who had a penchant for getting into constant trouble.

His lips curved into a cynical smile as he thought of his first motorcycle, a fire engine red 1975 Indian. Nick removed the baffle plates from the bike's exhaust muffler just to annoy the hell out of everyone with the noise. The personification of the bad biker dude, he'd been all attitude and presence on his red Indian. He spoke to no one and everyone got out of his way when he walked down the hall at school. Nick hated Rockland High. Talk about not fitting in. He wore black leather even back then.

One person he'd noticed was Ronnie Barnes. Two years younger than him, she'd been outgoing, gregarious, and popular and everything he wasn't. She had a killer body then and from what he observed three years ago at a distance, she still did.

While her glorious curves attracted his attention and stirred his raging teenage hormones, the intense feelings expanded beyond lust the more he'd observed her. Kind and generous with her friends, affectionate and teasing with her brother, she appealed to him in all ways. His first crush. Hell, his first serious bout of puppy love, unrequited though it had been.

Nick leaned on the counter and gazed outside into the parking lot of his small bar, The Chief. There stood the object of his current affection, his 2013 Dark Horse Indian, one of two motorcycles he owned. Damn, the bike was beautiful, all black and sleek with the tell-tale fringed leather seat. If anyone touched his baby, he would rip out their spine. The bike was parked where he could keep an eye on it while he worked in his bar.

His thoughts drifted back to Ronnie. Nick wasn't afraid of anyone or anything, then or now. However, Ronnie Barnes rendered him mute. For months he tried to screw up the courage to approach her and to talk to her, but by March of his senior year—he was gone.

The bakery was located at 35 Waterloo Street; if he remembered right it used to be a beauty parlor back in the day. Maybe he should check it out.

Suddenly, Nick felt as if he were back in high school. Why did Ronnie Barnes have him acting this way? The unsure teenager he used to be, which he thought he'd moved past. Not as far as she was concerned, apparently.

Over the years, there had been no shortage of women. One of Nick's rules since he lost his virginity at age sixteen was that he never slept with a woman more than once. Cold and calculating perhaps, but it worked so far. Sex to Nick was a necessity of life, like air or food, nothing more. He never once engaged his heart in his many encounters.

When did he last have sex? *Oh yeah*. He smiled knowingly. Four days ago he hooked up with a waitress at the Top Hat Diner. What a night. Is that what he wanted with Ronnie Barnes? A night of hot, wild sex? Swinging from the rafters, pounding, driving with plenty of raw, animal lust? Hell, yeah. Nick dreamed about sinking into her luscious body since his teens. He imagined how tight and wet she'd be when he'd finally get her under him. He hardened just thinking about it. His leather pants groaned in protest at his sudden erection. *Down boy*. Nick folded the flyer and stuffed it in his back pocket. Guess he'll be buying cookies or bread in three days' time. He watched as the Budweiser truck pulled into the parking lot to make his delivery. The time had come to get to work and push Ronnie Barnes out of his mind.

You can't go home again. These words haunted Veronica Barnes for weeks leading up to her return to her hometown.

She cocked her head and watched as the MacDougall company crane put into place the sign advertising the name of her new business, Titus Bakery. The temptation to call out to the workers that the sign didn't look level nagged at her, but surely these guys knew their business. After some measurements, the men did hang it to her satisfaction.

She scanned the front of the building. Not too large and kind of quaint with the old brick facade. This building had been around since the Twenties. The place was hers now, lock, stock, and worn bricks. The ceramic tile by the front entrance looked decades old, but was still in beautiful shape. The large store front windows were also a big plus. However, sun beating in on baked goods might not be a good idea. She would see about shaded glass or maybe refrigerated units for her cakes. Veronica pulled out her iPod Touch and typed reminders for later.

The unmistakable hum of a V-8 engine came up behind her. It had to be her brother, Tyler. Who else would be driving an obvious unmarked police cruiser? Tyler Barnes opened the door of the black Crown Victoria and leaned on the driver's side window.

"Hey sis, what in hell is this Titus Bakery? You're a Barnes again."

Veronica pushed her glasses up her nose; they had a habit of always slipping down no matter how many times through the years she bought new glasses. She slipped her iPod in her pocket, and then crossed her arms in mock annoyance. Tyler, her older brother by two years, was a detective with the Rockland Police Department. He was blond and at least six-one in height with a lean musculature a cover model would envy. He always spoke his mind, at least to her.

"I don't like the name Barnes Bakery. Besides, since I'm using the settlement money to start this venture, it seems fitting to call the place after Billy-boy Titus."

William Titus—her fourteen week mistake. A lesson learned. Hot, feral sex doesn't translate into a lasting love or marriage. She secretly wished it did. Caught up in the throes of a passionate, drunken weekend with rich, real-estate entrepreneur, William Fortesque Titus II, they'd wound up at one of those cheesy Vegas chapels that dot the strip. Thirty-six hours later, they'd realized their mistake.

Now divorced, she'd been given a check with an obscene amount of zeros on it. Sucking up her courage, she quit her consultant's job in San Francisco, California, and headed back home to Rockland, a small blue-collar city nestled on the Chesapeake across from Washington, D.C. Her brother was the only family remaining in town. Her father died three years ago, and her mother moved to Port Ritchie, Florida, to live with her older sister, Elmira, among the orange groves and alligators.

At twenty-nine, Veronica was ready for a little life change. She took a deep breath hoping to inhale some fresh air. Instead, she wrinkled her nose.

"Ewww, is that the pulp mill? It smells as bad as when I left."

Tyler shrugged. "I don't even smell it most days. Besides, it's always worse when it's hot and muggy like this."

This was hot? Tyler should've come out to California for a visit, she thought to herself.

Before she could speak, Tyler sighed at what he knew was Ronnie's unasked question. "Yes, I put someone trustworthy on getting the flyers out, slipped under doors, left on car windshields, yadda, yadda." He held up his hand to still her response. "Get that look off your face, I supervised. It was done to your exact directions. Besides, I shouldn't have done it all as it's actually illegal." He grinned mischievously.

Veronica hugged her brother tight.

"Thank you, I'm so nervous. The mixers and ovens were delivered this morning and Ty, I had no idea the flour's in seventy-five pound bags! How am I going to lift it?"

Tyler stepped back and placed his hands on her shoulders.

"Are you sure you're ready for the grand opening in three days? Have you even hired any help yet?"

"I can manage for a while until it gets off the ground." she replied.

"You've got the money, Ronnie, hire someone and fast. Damn, you told me with the baking alone you will be up at four in the morning. You can't put in fourteen hour days."

Veronica rolled her eyes. Tyler always ragged her ass since they were kids. But, she grudgingly had to admit the golden haired Adonis had a point.

"I'll call the employment agency. The reason I called you besides lifting the flour is I want you to inspect the rooms in back. I'll be living there."

Tyler's mouth dropped open. "Why? I said you could stay with me as long as you like. Why live in cramped rooms in back of the bakery? You'll never get away from the heat and the smell."

"There's nothing wrong with the smell of fresh baked goods. In fact, it's been proven no one gets angry in a bakery, the odor soothes people. Plus, they come in to purchase baked goods for happy occasions like birthdays and bar mitzvah's," Veronica laughed. "How can you have your lady friends over if your sister's there? I must be cramping your style at the moment. Of course, there were a few nights you didn't come home."

"I was on a stakeout. I told you," Tyler grumbled. "Now you sound like a wife."

"You know Mom is heartbroken. Last time we spoke she asked if you were seeing anyone serious. She's dying for beautiful, blond grandchildren, Ty."

"So, go ahead. Give her some," Tyler snapped.

"I touched a nerve. Sorry, Ty. Come on, let's go in and do an assessment. You can help me finalize my list of what products I'll be selling. I'll be starting with a just a few things, french bread, parker house rolls—"

"Cinnamon buns?" Tyler's face brightened. "Damn, you make the best cinnamon buns!"

Veronica laughed. She'd missed Tyler. Gone from Rockland, how many years? Wow, almost ten years except for a few visits and the funeral.

She missed her father deeply. How she would've loved to have him here helping, giving advice and hugs. Teagan Barnes had been a strapping, handsome man who hadn't been sick a day in his life until a heart attack took him away. His sudden death devastated them all, especially her mother. Veronica lifted her chin in determination. A new beginning, she was due.